penny candy

and Other Stories

Enjoy the Candy!

Trisha

D1302082

penny candy

and Other Stories

TRISHA BATCHELOR

October Writer Publishing

OCTOBER
WRITER

Philadelphia

Penny Candy and Other Stories. ©2019 by Trisha Batchelor

Published by October Writer Publishing
P. O. Box 12352
Philadelphia, PA 19119
www.octoberwriter.com

Manufactured in the United States of America

Interior Design by: Arlana Johnson

Cover Design by: Liz Demeter/Demeter Design

ISBN: 978-0-578-55870-7

For my parents

Daniel and Vivian

ACKNOWLEDGMENTS

My first thanks is to God. Thank you for holding the door open, and for reminding me that I can do all things through Christ who strengthens me.

These stories would have remained on dog-eared pieces of paper, or hidden deeply within old computer files, if it had not been for the encouragement of my husband Tony. I am better because of you.

I was inspired by my grandchildren Shawn, Austin, Sophia, Moriah, and Elle. My constant conversations with them regarding the importance of reading, pushed me to write. Each of you light up my life with a different color.

The unconditional love and constant cheerleading of my children Clenet, Larayne, and Eddie, has helped keep the flame of my imagination alive. You, my three little kittens, shall always have pie!

The professionalism, patience, and dedication of my editor Arlana Johnson contributed greatly to the success of this project. You are walking out the path set before you, and God is pleased.

And to Misty Gunter, for so many things that there is not room enough to write here, but that I cherish. You, my friend, are marvelous.

CONTENTS

JEALOUSY   1

MILLIE'S SONG   11

PENNY CANDY   23

MORE THAN LOVELY   29

RIGHTEOUS   77

THE STATION   91

PAUL AND SILAS   97

JEALOUSY

My big sister Tootsie left home when she was sixteen. The day she left, everybody acted surprised. But they really weren't. They knew she was going to leave, and so did I. I guess if they pretended about being surprised, then they could pretend they didn't have anything to do with it. She didn't say a word to nobody. Walked in from school, marched straight up the stairs and came back down in less than two minutes. She had her stuff in two black trash bags. On the way out she brushed past my mother, nice as you please. I was glad Tootsie got up the nerve to go, but while my heart was cheering her on, my mind was screaming, "Girl, you must be out of your mind!"

No one talked back to my mother, let alone try her like that. Plus, she could grab you real quick. I'd seen it many times and felt it too. But for some reason, this time my mother didn't reach out to snatch Tootsie up by the scruff of her neck. She watched her walk out the front door under the strain of those heavy bags. As the screen door banged shut, my mother whispered, "Don't you come back neither." I wanted to tell her that she didn't have to worry about that happening, but I wasn't crazy.

I once heard my Aunt Dee say that Tootsie wasn't much to look at, but even as a child I knew that was jealousy talking. Jealousy did a lot of talking in my family. I wish half of those who let jealousy talk for them would have spoken for themselves. We would have been much better off in the long run. Maybe then it would have been jealousy walking out the house that hot August day instead of my sister.

I have five siblings: three sisters and two brothers. Most of us have different fathers, and even those of us who have the same one don't favor each other in looks or demeanor. Challie is the oldest. He was born Charles Everett III. His father was Big Challie. We all had to call him Mr. Challie. One night when I was about six years old, my mother came into our room and squeezed into the bed between me and Tootsie. My other two sisters were asleep in the twin bed across from us. My mother said that she had something special to tell us. Cigarette smoke and the faint smell of alcohol laced her breath, but we didn't care. We wanted to know what this special thing was. Then, just above a whisper, she began to speak. She told us that Big Challie was her first love, and that if someone really loves you, then you would just know it. Something deep inside you would make you know it. She said that love was a matter of the heart, and your heart is connected to your stomach. You get butterflies in your stomach when you're in love, and when that love goes away, the butterflies die. When that happens, you feel empty. She fell asleep right there, with Tootsie and I on either side. That was it. That was the special thing she woke us up to say. Half of it wasn't news at all. Everybody knew our mother still loved Big Challie. The stuff about the stomach and the heart only helped me to understand why my mother hated butterflies.

I always thought that my brother's real name sounded grand. The way it rolled real slow off your tongue: Charles Everett III, like he was going to be rich one day. He was rich for two summers, or at least it seemed like he was. It didn't last long though, and neither did his car or that apartment he rented over on Braddock Street. All of that was taken away when Challie was hauled off to jail.

My sisters Tootsie and Retta have the same father, but I swear, you would never know that. Loudmouth Lauretta and quiet and reserved Tootsie. Now, their father was something to look at. I don't think I've ever seen nobody as handsome as Ricky Brewster. And I don't think I've met nobody as mean either. The first time I saw him slap my mother, she flew clear across the kitchen floor. That was the day I came face-to-face with heartbreak. I watched it well up in her eyes and spill over onto her cheeks. I learned that day that handsome don't mean a thing. As a matter of fact, if it meant anything, then it meant handsome has got to make you ugly so you don't have a chance of taking its shine. The uglier handsome makes you, the brighter it feels.

My brother Booker went by his last name. His government name was Soldier Man Booker. Only his teachers called him Soldier, something about it being "mandatory." His father never lived with us like all the others did. I could tell that made Booker sadder than he let on. All of our fathers lived with us at one time or another, even if their stays were short.

Booker told me he saw his father once, months after it happened. After Booker got around to telling me, I was mad that he didn't run into the house and get me that day. It happened the summer he turned ten, right outside our house when we lived on Livingston Avenue. He said my mother was leaning way too deep into the window of a burgundy Monte Carlo, the kind with the white vinyl half roof. He said his father wore a green army uniform, and he shook Booker's hand real hard. Booker said that his name was Wayne, and he seemed real nice, and that he was talking sweet to my mother. That part didn't mean nothing to me, though. Most men talked sweet to my mother.

Booker was proud to know that he looked just like his dad. He was happy they met because he would have never known where he got those freckles and that burnt orange hair, the same hair he got teased about his whole life. The hair that taught him how to fight. The hair that stood out no matter where he was. The hair that he tried to dye black when he was nine and made him look like a fool for six months. Black hair and bushy burnt orange eyebrows. He had a lot of fights at school during those months. But after Booker met his father that summer, he seemed pleased with his reddish-brown skin, freckled face, and orange hair. I wish I could have met his father too, but what really mattered was that Booker did. Everybody should know their daddy.

Free and me had the same father: Theophilus Lee Browning. That's a name for you. Our father stayed around the longest, but sometimes my mother would rotate the others back in. My sister Freeda Lee Browning was named after our daddy's mother, and I was named after my mother's hairdresser, Ms. Deena. Deena Rae Browning, that's my name.

So, there you have it. All spelled out on the branches of a crooked family tree: Challie, Retta, Tootsie, Booker, Free, and me, stairstep children born out of wedlock to my mother, Anita Lynn Hansberry. And no matter our various last names, to our neighbors we were "them Hansberry children." Inside the house we clashed like hot grease and water, except for me and Booker, of course. Outside of the house every-one knew that if you fought one of us, you chanced fighting us all.

Growing up, we lived in more than a few houses, but all in the same neighborhood. Every time we moved it was dark outside. One of those times, I walked up beside Retta, who was struggling to balance a stack of boxes, and I made the mistake of asking her why we couldn't move during the day. She gave me that mean "get out of my face" look and said that I should be more worried about the next place we were moving to and not about the time of day. She bumped me to the side and went on out the door. My mother never told us where we were moving to next. We never questioned it; just packed up our things at a moment's notice like we were told. Retta's reply had me worried. May-be it was just her mean self, trying to scare me. Retta and I were never close. She knew I was concerned about the next school I would be go-ing to and was probably just laying on her usual mental torture. This was my last year at Taylor Junior High and moving up to high school was a big deal. We lived four blocks from Doonesbury, and all of us Taylor eighth graders were supposed to go there in September. If we moved too far north, south, east, or west, I would no longer be in the district. That's why I hated Retta. She thrived on torturing you with the unknown.

Turns out we didn't leave the district. We could have just walked to the location of our next home, but my mother made us squeeze into the back seat of her car anyway. Retta's caution was not about school at all, it was about us moving to Carroll Street with Aunt Dee. Looking back, I would have preferred moving across town and attending Elling-ton, Fitzgerald, or Hughes Middle Schools. I would have fought nearly every day because I didn't know nobody, but I would have preferred that over living with Aunt Dee.

The house used to belong to our grandparents. They both died young. I think in their early fifties. My mother left the house when she was pregnant with Big Challie's baby. The young lovers moved atop Saltzman's Deli on Baker and Vine. Saltzman's is still there. Although the couple's first go-round lasted only a year, my mother didn't go back home to live with her parents and younger sister Dee. She worked two jobs—one of them at Saltzman's—and kept it moving, right into the arms of that handsome Ricky Brewster.

Aunt Dee never left home. She was the "good one," as my mother called her. She attended a local college, got a nursing degree, and was at home each night to care for their parents, who were both ravaged with cancer. Jealousy is a lot like cancer. It destroys relationships, breaks hearts, and made Tootsie leave home. It eats away at you on the inside and shows up on the outside. Just like cancer, it kills. Except one kills the body, the other the soul.

When we first moved in with Aunt Dee, I couldn't see it. The house was big. Aunt Dee slept in her childhood bedroom, my mother was in my grandparents' room, all the girls slept in a huge room on the second floor, and my brothers shared a bedroom on the third floor. Aunt Dee worked in the evenings at the hospital, so when we got home from school, she was pretty much on her way out the door. All the better for us, because she didn't like a lot of noise and always complained whenever we were laughing and having a good time. It's hard to live with your mother's rules and somebody else's.

Tootsie was my mother's favorite. We all knew it. Maybe it was because they looked so much alike, or because they had the same sense of style. Maybe it was because Tootsie did my mother's hair and knew more about her private life than the rest of us. Maybe it was because Tootsie didn't get along with Aunt Dee, just as my mother never did. Whatever the reason, Aunt Dee was well aware of their special relationship, and from the start did little things to wreck it. First of all, she told every time Tootsie came in past curfew, talked on the phone longer than the half hour we were allowed, or wore makeup to school. It wasn't that Aunt Dee didn't want to tell on the rest of us, but only Tootsie did those things. Still, she didn't have to tell on her.

My mother was strict on all of us—well, everybody but Challie. He was getting too old to be strict with. He had already lived on his own and was really only there until he could "get back on his feet," an expression it took me a while to understand. I saw him on his feet every day, eating up all the food in the house, not giving my mother any rent, and never doing any chores.

One time my mother found her favorite dress hanging on the bathroom door, hidden behind a robe, and naturally blamed Tootsie for trying to wear her clothes. Retta didn't wear sharp clothes like that, and me and Free were way too small. Tootsie denied it, but there was still a big argument. There was the time my mother could smell her own perfume in the house when she came in from work. Aunt Dee said it must have been Tootsie. Now, that one could have been Tootsie, because she loved to smell good. She got that honest. My mother always smelled better than anyone else in the room, but Tootsie denied that one too. Aunt Dee also blamed her when the brand-new hot curler set we all shared caught on fire because it was left plugged in too long. Then there was the morning the school called because Tootsie had been late. She had cramps the night before. I remember because she told me, but Aunt Dee told my mother she was dragging around the house and left late because she was primping in the mirror too long. It was one thing after another.

I wasn't sure what Aunt Dee had against Tootsie, but Tootsie knew that my mother couldn't afford a place of her own at the time. So she didn't let the accusations become a problem between the two sisters. Anyway, the heat was taken off of Tootsie for a while when Challie violated his parole and was sent back to prison. My mother took it hard. The only one that could console her was Big Challie. He didn't have to court her like others would have been required to do. He was Big Challie. So, she fell for him again. He started coming around a lot, and then he started sleeping there, right in my grandparent's bed. I loved my mother, and I was only a child, but even I felt funny about that. Challie began paying for my mother to go to the hairdresser and brought bags of food to the house once a week. It kept her mind off of losing her oldest son to the prison system yet again, but it came with a price.

With Challie gone, that left Booker alone on the third floor. My mother didn't allow boys and girls to sleep in the same room, but I spent a lot of nights up there with him. Since Booker had gained a new-found confidence in his skin and hair color, the phone never stopped ringing for him. Every time it rang, you could hear the disgust in the voice of whomever answered the phone. "Booker get the phone, boy," "Booker, one of your fresh-tailed friends is on the phone again," or "Booker you just used up your half hour! Sorry, he can't talk right now." Slam! Booker didn't care. The girls would still fall all over him at school.

It was in Booker's room late at night that we began to discuss the situation with my mother, Aunt Dee, and Tootsie. Booker told me that he thought Aunt Dee liked Tootsie in the wrong sort of way. The way Miss Anne across the street and her friend Tasha liked each other. Maybe that's why she was doing it. I told him flat out that he was crazy. He began comparing Aunt Dee to Retta and brought up all the ways they were alike. Mean spirited, condescending, hard on everybody, with no sense of style, and no smell of perfume. I told him he was really crazy then. I know Retta wasn't girly, but I heard about a few things. Marvin Slaughter and his cousin Dwayne Hallsboro from around on Beacon Street both liked Retta. I couldn't say why because it was a mystery to me, what with her boyish ways. But I knew it was true because Tootsie told me, and Tootsie never lied to me. We would go on like this for hours. It was like one of those detective novels Booker liked to read all the time. We were always trying to figure it out, and just when we thought we had, bam! We were wrong.

Big Challie was still sleeping in my grandparents' bed, and because we were at school during the day, we never saw much of his comings and goings. If my brother hadn't gotten himself locked up again, I bet he could have seen what we missed.

Ricky Brewster knew that my mother had taken up with Big Challie again, and although he was seeing some "two-bit whore" (that's what my mother called her), he still showed his face at our door now and then. He played like he was so interested in seeing Retta and Tootsie, but both of them were out chasing boys. When Ricky came past, he and my mother would sit on the porch and talk, usually Friday or Saturday nights when Big Challie was out doing whatever he did. It was jealously that brought him to the house those few times. Nothing ever really became of those sneak dates between Ricky Brewster and my mother. Maybe my mother was strong enough not to let handsome bring more heartbreak. Or maybe, although there was no longer outward evidence from all the beatings she took from him, the pain that was deep inside was enough to keep Ricky Brewster away. I told Booker it was the butterflies. Big Challie was back, and she was trying to keep the butterflies alive. He didn't understand, but not because he was stupid. I guess it was just that he wasn't a girl.

Aunt Dee used to sit inside the living room with the screen door open on those weekend nights. She watched old movies and gossiped on the phone. She didn't have a boyfriend at the time, and now my mother had two. One sleeping in their parents' bed almost every night, and one sitting on their parents' rusted green and white porch glider. Jealousy didn't have to try too hard to get a hold on Aunt Dee. It was easy, and my sister Tootsie was the one to recognize it.

The relationship between Tootsie and my mother was already strained. Tootsie looked like Ricky Brewster, just plain pretty, and she was his favorite child. Some say he had a few others scattered throughout the neighborhood. We never saw them. My mother both loved and hated Tootsie's pretty face. That alone was a deep-seated problem. With my mother believing that Tootsie was the one sneaking her clothes out of the house and wearing her perfume, it added fuel to the fire. The rest of us knew that it would only be a matter time before this thing blew up, and Tootsie would leave and go live with Ricky Brewster. It was unthinkable. Men left. But mothers and children stayed. They stayed together.

After Tootsie left and was settled in with her father and his girlfriend, I went around to visit her once. She lived on Beacon Street now, right next door to Marvin Slaughter, the one who liked Retta. I didn't tell my mother about the visit. It had been two weeks, but the wound was still too fresh. Only Booker knew, and he would have covered for me if needed. Tootsie is the one who told me all about jealousy, about how it was Aunt Dee who was wearing my mother's clothes and sneaking squirts of her favorite perfume. She saw Big Challie and Aunt Dee together more than once riding in his car. Aunt Dee had no idea. She blamed Tootsie for all that she was doing because she had to blame someone, and Tootsie was the perfect pick. Tootsie didn't want to tell my mother, not about the clothes and perfume, and certainly not about

Jealousy

Big Challie. She only told me and made me swear to keep it. Tootsie believed that Big Challie was the lesser of two evils in my mother's life. He was keeping Ricky Brewster away from our house and that meant no black eyes or busted lips for our mother. Tootsie didn't like Regina much—that was the girlfriend's name—but she only had a year left of high school, and she would be off on her own. Maybe my brother Challie would be out by then and they could get a place together.

I left my visit with Tootsie understanding that jealousy was a low-down dirty thing. A thing that could make you hurt even the people you were supposed to love. Although my mother knew she didn't want Ricky Brewster dragging her across our kitchen floor every night, and already had Big Challie sleeping in her parents' bed, she was jealous of Regina. Ricky Brewster had Regina to beat on now, but was jealous of where Big Challie was laying his head at night. Big Challie pretended he didn't know my mother was gliding on that rusty porch chair with Ricky Brewster, but he did, and jealously drove him to start talking sweet to Aunt Dee. Then there was Aunt Dee.

Aunt Dee didn't have the burden of six children she could barely feed. She had a nursing degree and worked at one of the best hospitals in the city. She never found herself three months behind on her rent, having to flee in the middle of the night to avoid being thrown out. Jealousy somehow gave her the notion that my mother's life was one to be desired. Jealously drove her to lay down with my mother's first love, to come between a mother and her child.

Tootsie didn't have to make me swear to keep it. I knew that I could never share with Booker what Aunt Dee had done. Let him keep thinking that Aunt Dee, Miss Anne, and her friend Tasha were meeting up at night.

I tip-toed up the stairs when I got home and went straight to my room. Thankfully Retta and Free weren't there. As I lay on the bed and thought about jealousy, heartbreak came to visit again. It welled up in my eyes and spilled over onto my cheeks. My stomach felt empty. My family was my first love, and the butterflies had died.

MILLIE'S SONG

Millie sat at the cracked mirror and wiped the pasty makeup from her face; first the left side, then the right. Slow, hard downward strokes—almost as if trying to remove the skin beneath. The tears that fell helped in the effort and actually had a much better effect than the cold cream she used religiously. Night after night, the same routine. The dressing room she shared with the ten or so other girls who worked at Harry's was dimly lit and uncomfortably small. It reeked with the smell of cigarettes, cheap perfume, regret, and a large dose of desperation. A few tiny, clear bags, the kind that once held fine crystals of cocaine, were mixed among the cosmetics scattered across the dressing table. Millie looked down at them feeling a twinge of hopelessness. White dust lined the inside of one and she quickly lifted her eyes to avoid its attraction. The flow of her tears seemed to quicken as she shifted her glance from the bags to her reflection in the mirror and back again.

"Tonight's sets seemed longer than usual for a Saturday night," she thought as she roughly brushed her wavy hair. The audience had chattered and laughed around her as she belted out tunes from the likes of Billie Holiday and Ella Fitzgerald. She tried her hardest to not let it affect her, but it was hard to ignore even the slightest level of disregard.

The clientele at Harry's had gradually changed over the last two years. What was once a vibrant nightclub for couples on dates, or friends looking for a fun night out, had turned into nothing more than a seedy Harlem bar. Her thoughts were interrupted when Blanche slung back the worn pink curtain that served as the dressing room door and floated in. She reached for one of the scattered tubes of lipstick on the dressing table. Millie always felt that Blanche was overly dramatic and drastically over-dressed, even for a lounge singer. Blanche quickly reapplied a few swipes of Lady Luck Ruby Red #2 and whipped around to return to the stage. Just as she reached the curtain, she turned.

"Cryin' ain't never done me no good, girl, and will more than likely treat you the same. Now put them bags in the trash before somebody tells Harry, and you go home penniless tonight. You know how he feels about drugs in his place."

Millie adjusted herself on the stool and shot back, "This stuff is not mine!"

But Blanche was gone. Millie collected the plastic bags to throw them away. She looked at the clock on the wall and quickly removed the remaining makeup from her face, wiped her eyes, and dressed to go home.

On her way out, she walked along the far wall of the club, looking back over her shoulder at Blanche, who was, as usual, theatrically ending her set. She could see Harry just to the right of the stage sitting upfront at his table. He said he liked to have a bird's-eye view of the place so he could watch the stage, the door, the bar, and the money. Millie stopped to collect her pay from Warren, the one-eyed bartender, and slipped out onto 125th Street.

The late-night breeze felt inviting. When she arrived at the club each evening, the sun was usually just setting, nestling down behind the jagged rooftops of the neighborhood buildings. When she walked home at night, the darkness always greeted her with emptiness, but for some reason this night felt different. The moon sat high in the heavens and lit her path with midnight hope. Tonight had been the first time she was able to resist opening one of those plastic bags, digging into the corners with her fingernail to get the last remnants of cocaine. It would have been completely normal for her to have wiped the remaining powder briskly across her gums. But not this night.

As she headed home, Millie passed by familiar people and places. A few of the hookers that made it their business to taunt her nightly with recommendations that she join them and make some real money, gave her room on the sidewalk as she passed. Millie peered back at them as she crossed over Lexington. Stray dogs that frequented the alleys didn't sheepishly approach her in hopes of a morsel of food, as was their normal routine. Tonight, they let her be. Even the nasty men who stood outside the Julep Bar tipped their hats and smiled. Yes, even those drunken fools who often made rude remarks during her sets. When they came to Harry's, they didn't do much listening. They preferred watching.

As she continued on her way, Millie thought about what she'd said to God a few weeks before. That night, she cried so hard at her bedside that she passed out. She hoped God had heard her before everything went black.

"God, give me one more chance. I know I don't deserve it, but without You I won't make it. I can't do this by myself. I can't let this go on my own!"

Those words came out like a guttural cry from the depths of her soul. It was like a circuit breaker snapped. Caught up in remembering her recent plea to God, she tripped over a pair of legs and nearly fell on her face. Sweet was sprawled out on the steps of her apartment building with his long legs extended onto the sidewalk.

"Sweet," she called down to him. "Sweet, get up."

Their paths crossed a long time ago in much the same way. That first night, it was compassion that compelled her to give him something to eat and let him sleep inside the hallway of the building. Every now and then, she would arrive home to find him there. She was usually the last tenant in at night. Sweet moved on by early morning, so no one ever knew. He seemed to be harmless. Far too young to be this down on his luck, but who was she to question his situation? Her friends called her stupid for letting a wino into the building and cautioned that she'd be sorry sooner or later.

Sweet didn't want anything to eat tonight. He thanked her as usual, gave his signature wink, and huddled up into a ball.

Morning arrived. Sunlight poured through Millie's window and splashed against the walls. Millie felt like a well-watered plant—strong, straight, and bright. God was answering her prayer. He was healing her.

She lay across the bed, relaxed, allowing the natural light to bathe her in its warmth. In the next moment she was jolted by the shrieking voice of her landlord, Ms. Adelle. Running to the window, she looked out over the street just in time to see Sweet's feet hit the curb. As he ran across the street, Ms. Adelle was fast on his heels with broom in hand. In mid-stride, he turned, looked up toward Millie's third-floor window and winked. She shrunk back from the window to avoid being seen.

Thaddeus Alabama Sweet was his name. His family called him Sweet for as long he could remember. His mother started that up and everyone else just followed suit. He was the youngest of seven children born to Albert Joseph and Ada Lee Sweet. He came from church folk from way back. Praying people. Grandma Lou taught him how to pray. His siblings Ruth, Daniel, Isaiah, Noah, Mary and John all favored his father's people. They were true Sweets through and through. Brown, round, and five feet from the ground. That's how people in town affectionately referred to them. Sweet's make up couldn't be more different. He was the color of rich peanut butter, every bit of 6 feet 5 inches, and had hands the size of frying pans. His teeth were straight, but his smile was crooked. His siblings often teased him but knew not to go too far. They knew he had something special, believed what their Grandma often said about him: "God done visited this boy."

At the age of ten, he prayed his brother Noah back to his feet when he fell into a grave meant for old man Clancy and broke his legs. Doctors said Noah would never walk again. Sweet said, "The devil is a lie!" At twelve he prayed his classmate Sinclair Lundy back to full hearing when she went deaf due to a fever that ran over 107 degrees for more than a week. At fourteen he even prayed the church out of a financial bind when he heard grown folks talking about possibly losing the building. What was true, and everyone knew it, was plain and simple: Sweet believed God!

At sixteen, Grandma Lou got sick. She cautioned him that

this time praying for her was not the answer. God was calling her home. Before Sweet turned seventeen, she was gone. He did not scream and holler at the funeral like his sisters. He didn't tear at Grandma's lavender dress as she lay in the casket like his father had. He also didn't try to jump in the grave at the cemetery like his brothers had done. No, Sweet sat right in the front row during the service, smiled at his Grandma Lou, and thanked God she'd been part of his life. Because he was the only one in her room when she died, everyone was curious about what she said before she passed. Everyone wanted to ask him, but most were afraid. At age eighteen, when Sweet was preparing to leave Maryland for New York, his mother finally got up the nerve.

"Sweet," she asked, taking his face in her hands. "What did Grandma Lou say to you before she went to be with the Lord?"
Sweet smiled his crooked smile.

"She prayed with me, mom. She told me to remember that God always hears prayer. Then she winked at me and said she would see me soon."

It was getting harder for Millie to walk into Harry's each evening. When she first began working there she was a strung-out drug addict, a young woman who had allowed men to dominate her decisions and leave when they no longer had any use for her. A scared little girl who snorted cocaine because her boyfriend did, and couldn't stop for fear that she would lose him. Millie was no longer that person anymore. Yes, she had earned easy wages at Harry's, but that didn't mean she owed him or anyone else anything. She still had her college degree. Although unused to date, it was still hers. No number of men or amount of drugs could take that away. She never took advantage of the education her parents had worked so hard to provide for her. Straight out of college, she ran into the arms of one loser after another, each one promising bigger dreams than the next. Not one ever delivered. Her addiction snuck up on her. She only meant to use the drugs occasionally, or socially, as it was called in some circles. Soon occasionally became week-ly and then daily.

Benny didn't introduce her to drugs. Millie alone took the blame for that. She experimented a little as a rebellious teenager and so didn't fear trying newer, more illicit substances. Benny was her cata-lyst to self-hatred. He was a verbally abusive, coked up, poor excuse for a man who stripped her of her self-esteem and made her too ashamed to associate with her friends and family. Once she lost control of her mind, her body followed and then her very soul. Alienated from every-one who really loved her, he was all she had. She stayed with him for close to five years, and those years included the three times he left her for someone else. There was always someone else. But he always came back, and she always gave in. Her head was hung too low to look in the mirror and see her deterioration. A male friend of theirs once told her something that turned out to be very true.

"He can leave you a thousand times and come back. You two will never be over until you leave him. That's when it will be done."

That's all the friend ever said on the subject. He never had an opinion on their relationship before then and never mentioned it after. At that time, she managed to hold down a job as an administrative as-sistant with a prestigious law firm in town. She hid her addiction behind dark glasses and excuses. Eventually they let her go. Being an addict, even a functioning one, always took over. She walked out of the office that day expecting everything to be alright, but how wrong she was.

Unemployment, food stamps and a visit or two to the free clin-ic showed her that everything was far from alright. Benny didn't help financially. He never had. Every dime he made doing odd jobs went up his nose. Before now she hadn't paid that much attention to his lack of financial support. She was too busy getting high herself.

That's how she found her way to Harry's Club. Because she couldn't pay the rent, she was put out of her downtown apartment and stayed with a friend for a short time. She knew the arrangement was only temporary. A girl she got high with every now and then told her Harry's was hiring dancers. Millie was no dancer, but she could sing. She walked in uninvited and unrehearsed, but to her surprise, Harry hired her on the spot.

The customers loved Millie, and the more drinks Harry sold, the more her pay increased. Harry was good that way. She was able to get a small apartment on the third floor of a nice brownstone. The first year or so didn't seem that hard. She had a routine. Sleep all day, get high with Benny in the evenings, and sing four sets at Harry's each night. She was drifting through life while marching toward death. Benny had not left her for anyone during that time. It was a strange feeling because he normally left so often, she was really looking forward to the break. She didn't get high when he was gone. She often wondered if she was really addicted to Benny, and not the cocaine.

Finally, the day came. Benny hadn't done anything different. He was just as verbally abusive and good for nothing as he had always been. There were no late nights out, or girls calling him at all hours. He had gone to his brother's house to watch a basketball game. When he returned everything—every single belonging he had at Millie's apartment—was sitting on the sidewalk. It happened just that quickly. She wasn't sure why or how, but she got up the nerve to say goodbye. She walked around the apartment gathering his things into trash bags, tears streaming down her face, memories running through her mind of every hurt he had inflicted on her, every hateful word he heaped on her head, every time he lied to her, cheated on her, and disrespected her. How had she let it go on so long? Where had the Millie her parents raised been while all this was happening?

The landlord's brother, Sam, lived in the building next door. He served as the handyman for all of Ms. Adelle's properties. At Millie's request he was changing her locks. Sam explained that he couldn't do anything about the main door, because it would cause too much trouble for the other tenants. Millie didn't care. The physical locks were only a formality. It was the door to her heart that she had to make sure Benny never entered again. Benny stood on the sidewalk beneath her window and spewed curses for forty-five minutes. Millie was surprised that no one called the police. His bicycle was lying on a heap of garbage bags, with a few boxes. Eventually the cursing morphed into unnatural laughter. She stood in the window looking down at him. There were no words needed. The Bible says laughter is like good medicine. But Benny never read the Bible, so he didn't know that his laughter didn't hurt Millie. It restored her.

Millie sang at Harry's one last time after Blanche all but accused her of owning those coke bags in the dressing room. She realized that preparing for sets in a dressing room full of drugs and women who were still addicted wasn't such a good idea. Stopping wasn't good enough. She had to remove herself from the destructive environment she had put herself in. She gave Blanche a big squeeze on the way out. It felt kind of silly because she had never hugged her before, but at the same time it felt right. Blanche had been more like a den mother than another nightclub singer. She never touched drugs, only counseled or consoled. Millie was so focused on taking that last walk along the bar and out the door that she didn't even notice Warren's outstretched hand trying to give her the pay envelope. She left without it.

Millie took a cab home from Harry's for the first time ever that night. The ride was so short the cabbie caught an attitude when she told him the address. By the time she settled in her seat, it was time to get out. And there he was, just as he had been on so many other nights.

Sweet lay across the second step of her apartment building with his legs stretched across the pavement. Instead of tapping him on her way in, with the intent of offering him shelter for the night, she sat down on the step near his head. She'd never really gotten a good look at Sweet. She only saw him at night, and by morning he was always gone. But tonight, he held her interest. She was not stumbling in this time. She was not stinking drunk from too many vodka tonics or steaming mad from something Benny had done. All those things, which had previously clouded her mind and weighed down her spirit were now in the past. Who was this man who lay on her steps more often than she could remember? Where did he stay when he wasn't here?

She wasn't seated long before he opened his eyes and stared

straight into hers. She should have been startled, but wasn't. He didn't say a word. He allowed her to really take him in. He knew this was the first time she had ever really bothered to look. He also knew this was the first time she had the heart to. Millie stared at his feet. Not sure why, she just did. His brown boots weren't worn or dirty. His clothes were layered, but oddly enough not tattered or rank. The dark brown knitted hat he wore contrasted starkly against his complexion. His eyes were soft and warm. And to Millie's surprise, he was a very young man, much younger than herself. Her trance was broken when he began to speak.

"When we met on these steps close to a year ago, you never asked me more than my name, and gave me yours. You never told me to go away, just let me in and saw to it that I had something to eat and a warm place to lay my head. You laughed with me every time I had to haul tail from your landlady."

He smiled hard at that, and so did Millie. She wanted to jump in and say so many things. Tell him why she never bothered to have a conversation before, explain that her life was so broken that she didn't have time for anyone else's problems until now. He could tell where she was going and put a single finger to his lips.

"I guess you realize now that I'm not who or what others perceive me to be. I'm not a drunk. I'm not useless, or lazy, or dangerous. I'm also not homeless, and definitely not hopeless. Millie Renee Redding..."

Millie drew back from him and jumped to her feet. Now that was enough! She may have been able to handle the fact that the "old man" she and every one of her friends thought was a wino, was really young and very handsome, but this was too much. How did he know her full name? Ms. Adelle never posted names on the mailboxes in the hallway, only the apartment numbers. Sweet's expression didn't change. He didn't react to her quick movements or her rise from the steps. He just relaxed, looked up at her and continued.

"Millie Renee Redding, God sent me here to this very stoop to pray. At first I didn't know why or for whom."

Millie slowly sat back down on the steps and gave Sweet her

undivided attention. Her eyes welled up with water, so much so that the tears clouded her sight until they finally poured down onto her cheeks. Sweet reached out to catch a tear just before it dropped from her chin and continued again.

"Others who live in this building never had a kind word for me, never once offered me so much as a cup of water. They called me names and even threw things at me a time or two, but not you. I watched you night after night, smelled the liquor on your breath as you told me to wake up and come inside. I saw the pain in your eyes as you stood right up there in that window and watched your boyfriend leave you more than once. I could hear your heart breaking. Then I realized God sent me here to pray for you."

Sweet stood and took Millie's hands, bringing her to her feet.

"You see Millie, when you didn't have the strength to fight or believe, I believed God for you."

She was overtaken with sobs. She reached for the railing to steady herself and pushed over a trash can instead. Sweet grabbed her by the arm to help. It was late, and all the racket had drawn Ms. Adelle to her open window. She raised her hand in a threatening motion.

"If you don't get from around here! Stay away from my place, boy!" she screamed.

With that, she slammed the window closed. It didn't seem as though she even saw Millie standing there with her hands in Sweet's. They looked each other square in the eyes. No blinking. No distractions.

"I have to go now," he said gently, taking her face in his hands. "But know this. God sent me to pray, but it was Him who heard your cries and calmed your storm. Your latter days will be greater than your past Millie. I mean...Millie Renee Redding."

They both laughed softly.

"I'm being called to someone else," he whispered as he began to back away.

Millie couldn't move. All this time she hadn't been able to utter a single word. She was stuck somewhere between sadness and joy. She was amazed at all she had heard, but was fighting against a sadness she didn't understand.

"Sweet," she was finally able to whisper, hardly able to get the word out. He had backed off of the curb and was standing a couple of feet into the street.

"That's it? Now you just leave?"

He smiled his crooked smile, winked at her and answered.

"Remember, God always hears you. I'll see you soon." And then he was gone.

PENNY CANDY

As the little girl rounded the corner, she could see her destination just a block away. A steady influx of children converged upon Vick's corner store, tucked tightly below the first floor of a row home. As she grew closer, her eyes widened, and her mouth began to water. This was similar to the reactions of all the schoolchildren as they approached the neighborhood establishment. The proprietor could not have chosen a more profitable location if he had tried. The store sat at an intersection that was along the route for children who attended the local elementary and junior high schools.

The little girl's ill-fitting school uniform held one shallow pocket, conveniently located at her right side. Normally the pocket contained a single dime for chocolate milk at lunch, and on Wednesdays, an extra dime for a soft pretzel. Because she achieved straight A's the prior semester, she had won the coveted privilege of being a school Pretzel Girl, delivering brown bags of pretzels to the classrooms each week. This also came with the perk of one free pretzel for herself. Today, however, was special. Her shallow pocket was weighed down by a handful of shiny coins. The extra load made her clothes look lopsided. Her waistband hiked up on one side, pinching at her ribcage. A grin stretched across her face, and as she walked the jumble of coins bounced against her hip in a melodic rhythm. She knew that today would be different.

Going to Vick's was not a rare occasion for her. She often accompanied her friends there as they went through their ritualistic selection of penny candy. Vick or some other member of his family would stare the children down as they methodically picked out their choices for the day. This job was meant for the extremely patient, to say the least. Today was special because her father, who did not live with her, had given her the coins the night before. She didn't see him often, but every time she did, she was elated. The worst times were when he and her mother were at odds. They would never have violent arguments, but their hushed disagreements behind closed doors could be overheard. "You're a liar!" "Stop acting crazy." "Get out!" "I'm not coming back."

She would lay on her bed cringing, knees bent toward her chest, listening to the verbal clashing and barrage of mean words. The consequence was always the same: "Your daddy won't be back anytime soon."

Today, with the change her father had given her, it was her turn to ride into Vick's on a high horse to select her favorite candies. Then she would exit the store triumphantly with her bounty nestled in a small brown bag. As she approached the corner, her thoughts drifted, and she briefly lost the rhythm of her stride. The once merry hop relaxed, and she became sullen.

"Wait a minute," she said aloud. "Why did he give me so many coins this morning? I wonder if he...if he's coming back this time."

Small beads of perspiration began to form at her hairline. A look of panic washed across her face, and her stomach began to ache. Within seconds she stepped up onto the curb in front of the store. Her small hand grew damp as she squeezed the coins in her pocket.

Again, she thought aloud, "What should I do?"

Her purposeful gait toward Vick's began to falter. The dilemma caused her to stand still right in the middle of a wild twister. Children were racing all around her on the sidewalk. Some screaming, "hunks!", a neighborhood term that allowed them sharing rights to the candy bags of their friends. Others rushed from the store stuffing small brown bags into pockets and compartments, to avoid having to share. A small tussle broke out between two boys as they attempted to split a box of Lemonheads. The hurried activity resembled grownups at a farmer's market, buying and bartering wares.

She leaned against the glass door and squeezed through, as children pushed past her on their way out. A small bell secured by a thin ribbon rang out as the door allowed pint-sized patrons to enter and exit the candy heaven. The morning sunlight poured into the dimly lit space, and before she realized it, there she was, standing at the edge of the glass counter. Sweat had begun to roll down her neck and then her back. Her hand hurt as the coins dug deeply into her palm.

"Well?" someone said from behind the counter. She didn't move. Couldn't move. She just stood there looking down at her pocket.

"Well?" The second plea for her order somehow reached her ears. She looked up.

"Whatcha gonna get?"

She quickly tried to remedy the problem, thinking, "Spend all the money, and he'll have to come back, or hold onto it because he's not coming back."

Before she knew it, she blurted, "I'll take ten Squirrel Nuts, five Red Hot Dollars, ten Shoe Strings, five Mary Janes, ten Grape Twisters, a box of pumpkin seeds, a bag of Sugar Babies, a Sugar Daddy, five Peanut Chews, and some Mike and Ike's."

It was Vick taking the order. He twisted his lips and said, "Let me see your money."

One by one the little girl placed the moist coins on the counter. In her attempt to separate a nickel from a dime, the dime flew across the counter and spun on its edge. Vick smacked it down with his hand. "Well I guess you got it," he said, surprised.

Once outside the store she stuffed the small brown bag into her lunch box. She was worn out. The candy-buying frenzy had left her discontented. Unlike the other children, she didn't know when the opportunity would present itself again to go on such a spree. She was still uncertain whether her father was coming back. Her stomach began to hurt again, but she fixed her face like a stone and walked into the school.

Later that evening, she watched her mother closely for signs that a truce may have occurred between her parents. There was none. Her mother was neither happy nor sad. Asking about it was unheard of. It was grown folks' business. Before she went to bed that night, she peeked into her small rumpled bag to take inventory of the remaining candy: seven Squirrel Nuts, one Red Hot Dollar, five Shoe Strings, four Mary Janes, two Grape Twisters, the box of pumpkin seeds, a half bag of Sugar Babies, a Sugar Daddy, and two Peanut Chews. She ate the whole box of Mike and Ike's at lunch. Shoe Strings and Grape Twisters were her favorites, so they wouldn't make it through the next day or two. She would try her best to ration the rest.

On Monday morning, just before leaving for school, the phone rang. Her mother sat at the kitchen table drinking tea and eating toast. She didn't move. The little girl didn't get phone calls, so she knew better than to reach for it. The ringing stopped and started again. She began chewing on her lower lip. Her mother busied herself with her morning routine, packing lunch and standing at the freezer deciding what to take out for dinner.

"Why does she seem so unconcerned?" she questioned silently. "How can she not wonder if it's him and if he wants to come over?"

The phone began ringing for a third time, and before she knew it, she picked up the receiver.

"Hello?" she managed to utter. She watched her mother's face, trying to estimate her level of anger for this defiant act.

"Hey Peanut," her father replied. His voice was tender and wonderful.

In the week following the bold telephone move, the little girl did not see or hear from her father. The time had passed without his voice, his hugs, or his laughter. Her parents had never shared the same home, and now they weren't sharing the same bed, even if only once a week. Her father's name was not mentioned, but the lack of his presence—however brief—was constantly visible in her mother's eyes.

Then, suddenly, one night a call came.

The little girl tried hard to focus on her schoolwork. She maintained periodic eye contact with her teacher so as not to be found out. Her attention was secretly drawn to the tall windows that lined one side of the classroom. It was now late spring. The time of year when the windows were opened wide as the school year neared its end. A cool breeze drifted around the room. When called on to answer a question, the correct answer sat on the little girl's tongue and rolled out of her mouth with fluidity. She never had to worry about being lost when it was her turn to read aloud or complete a problem on the board. Those were not her worries.

The clock finally released its hold on time and struck noon. The children lined the walls, preparing to exit the doors for the journey home. She had no intention of walking home today. As the doors flew open, the warm afternoon air greeted the children. A few girls announced their after-lunch Double Dutch partners. Others spread out across the schoolyard. She heard a few kids bragging about their plans to stop at Vick's. This announcement caused those with and without change in their pockets to form a caravan and head toward the store.

Above the voices and through the crowds, the little girl spotted the reason for her anxiousness. On the other side of the tall cyclone fence, a white Oldsmobile with a shiny black vinyl roof sat at the curb with the motor running. The sun shone so brightly that others couldn't see who was inside. But she knew. The person in the car was there for her. Delight overtook her as she ran toward the opening in the fence. She leaned inside the passenger side window and focused on his face. Handsome. Brown.

The ride home was a mere seven blocks away, a stone's throw for an inner-city child. But today it felt like a ride across town. As she sat low in the front seat, sometimes raising up to lean out of the open window to catch the breeze, he drove slowly, rounded corners patiently, allowing the few traffic lights they met to catch him on red.

He handed her a thin heavy canvas bag full of loose change and allowed her to fill her fist with as much as she could hold. They laughed playfully as she tried to take more than she could manage, dropping a few dimes and nickels onto her lap. Visions of her next visit to Vick's floated through her mind: Twisters, Mary Janes, Red Hot Dollars, and Shoe Strings. Oh yes, Shoe Strings!

When they arrived at her street, the large leafy trees welcomed them like old friends who were sharing in this cherished moment. She grabbed her father's strong shoulder and pulled herself up from the seat, resting her knees on the cool leather. She reached over and hugged his neck tightly, kissing his brown whiskered cheek. He didn't go into the house with her. She didn't expect or need him to.

The fact that she may or may not see him the next day or the day after that did not worry her anymore. She skipped up the steps, reached for the door key that hung on a chain from her neck and opened the front door. As if in slow motion, she turned and waved goodbye. The sun was still shining brightly, so she could no longer see his face, but she knew he could see hers. With that, the shiny white Oldsmobile slowly rolled down the street.

When she returned to the schoolyard after lunch, the little girl had a jump rope partner. She played with the other children and shared candy she'd picked up on her way back to school. Playtime soon ended, and they all filed back into the classroom. She sat in her seat near the open windows. The breeze caressed her face, gently touching the places her father's whiskers had pricked her soft skin. She looked down at her balled fist and smiled. Although the money was gone, she still squeezed tightly, holding onto something much more precious.

MORE THAN LOVELY

S ummer has always been sweet for me. It's not just the fact that bulky, often ill-fitting coats can be stashed away in storage closets. It's the familiar scents that slip past your nostrils without notice, yet somehow manage to rest deep down in your soul and awaken your memory.

Many of my childhood summers were spent at my grand-mother's house in North Carolina. Every year right after school let out, a pattern of energetic chattering would begin to stir in my house as my mother prepared me for the trip.

"Change your clothes every day. You hear me, Cecely?" she would say. "And don't be a bother."

My mother brought me up right, and these two things were standard behavior for me. She knew that I knew this, but each year she continued to remind me. I would sit on the edge of my bed during these ritualistic clothes-packing sessions and received, with closed-mouth obedience, my instructions for what would be another marvelous summer.

"Now each set is stacked just so. Wear the set like it's stacked. You hear me Cecely?"

I had long ago become accustomed to my mother making a comment and then asking if I'd heard it even though she required no answer. I watched her closely each year during this time. As the summers came and went, she never seemed to age. She placed each item into my traveling case, and as she packed the clothing, her hand would brush across the fabric. Her words were sharp and swift as her head moved about. Her large, almond-shaped eyes perusing my room, the drawers of the dressing table, being sure nothing was forgotten.

"Your Uncle Shot has been sick most of the winter, so he won't seem much like his old self. Let him be. He needs his strength to help Mother out. You understand, Cecely?"

Her hair was pulled back, tied in a ponytail that started at the nape of her neck and worked its way down just past her shoulders. One wisp fell loosely from her temple and brushed across her butterscotch cheek. Eventually, the hair began to annoy her and she pushed it back behind her ear. This was the way each of my summer adventures to North Carolina began.

"Are you going to block the pavement all day, or do you have other plans?"

Chacho, my first-floor tenant abruptly stopped his bicycle behind me and startled me out of my daydream. I was holding my grocery bag much too loosely, and fruit began to spill onto the ground.

"Chacho!" I screamed in part annoyance and part laughter, bending down in an attempt to grab a rolling orange.

"Wake up, girl!" he hollered back as we scurried along the curb chasing a few runaway lemons. "Get it together," he admonished after all the produce was retrieved. "I realize Harlem has been hailed in these trendy magazines as upscale nowadays, but you can still get knocked upside your head!"

The bag held tightly now, I gazed up at the evening sky. "I was just taking in the scents of summer. Can't you smell it? Just try, you might..."

With my back to Chacho, I hadn't noticed that he all but ignored me as he lifted his bicycle and carried it up the steps and into the building.

"Come on," he shouted over his shoulder. "If you want to talk to me, my dear, you're gonna have to come inside."

When I first rented out the apartment below me to Chacho, I was more than curious when he printed his name on the rental application as merely CHACHO. That's it. No last name. And yes, in all capital letters. This was my first cue as a new landlord to ask for a valid piece of identification. His New York driver's license could not accommodate the length of his full name and only included, "Carlos H. A. C. H. Ortega." Although he will deny it to this day, he snatched back the license from my hand, as if I was to blame for the New York Department of Transportation's actions. He then rolled his eyes harder than any teenaged girl I had grown up with, leaned to one side, and looked me in my eyes.

"It's like I said, and as the application states Ms. Dodd, my name is Chacho. Now if you have the breath to say my name each time we speak, then feel free. My mother, rest her soul, named me after her many brothers and closed it out with the last name of a man I never had the pleasure of meeting. She, herself, only shared a brief moment with him, if you know what I mean." With that he flashed an adorable smile.

"My given name is Carlos Humberto Andriez Cristobal Horacio Ortega. And since in my family it would be disrespectful to cut out any one uncle and allow another to remain, I call myself Chacho. I would prefer that you do the same."

Had it not been for the fact that he was the only employed person who replied to my "Apartment for Rent" sign, our meeting would have ended right there. But to tell you the truth, I knew there was more to Chacho than that. Though loud and obnoxious, he came across as down to earth and refreshing. His hair was more pulled together than mine and his clothes told me he had a great sense of style that I could learn from. So what if he had an attitude? He had references!

With the fallen fruit stored safely in my refrigerator, I went downstairs to Chacho's for a bite to eat. Through the blaring sounds of Tito Fuentes, Chacho and I laughed and ate the greasy tacos he'd made from scratch the day before.

"I'm going to get out of these street clothes and make myself comfortable. Be right back," he said as he walked toward his bedroom. I rested my head on his way-too-soft and way-too-green couch and thought about whether I wanted to go to Lovely's funeral. It was not until Saturday, but I had already made a running list of excuses ever since my mother told me Sunday night. I hadn't been to North Carolina in years and hadn't seen Lovely in all that time. When Chacho returned to the living room, comfortable turned out to be the old baby blue terry cloth sweat suit I asked him to drop off at the Goodwill last week. This was classic Chacho, so I didn't waste my breath complaining. I had to admit, he looked better in it than I ever did.

"So, are you going or not?" he shouted over the music, leaning to turn the volume down. "Work is not a factor since school let out, and you have no man to speak of since you let that last disaster go."

I poked out my bottom lip and hung my head, but couldn't hold back the smile.

"So what's it gonna be?"

"It's not about work, although I was thinking about helping out with the summer program. And I'll have you to know that I recently agreed to go out with Brenda's cousin, Charles. You know, cute Charles." I collected the plates from the coffee table and walked them over to the kitchen sink.

"Stop it! Your excuses are tired, and so am I. Some of us have to go to work in the morning."

He followed me to the sink and bumped my hip to move me out of his way.

"I've got these dishes. Go on home and make up your mind." He waved me away from the kitchen.

I grabbed my throw blanket off the couch and gathered my phone and keys.

"You know me too well," I said. "It's not about any of those things. I just don't know if I can do it. Lovely and I were best friends for a very long time. Yeah, it was years ago, but every memory I have of her is warm and pleasant. I don't know if I want the last one to be of her lying in a casket."

Chacho gently pushed me toward the door. "Sounds nostalgic

and all, but you can't have your mother's calls forwarded to me one more day. Make up your mind. Chacho is no secretary. It's hard work being me, and there's no time for much else."

I shoved his shoulder as I backed out the door. "You are out of your mind. You know that?"

He rolled his eyes and closed the door. I realized how deep our friendship had grown over the past few years. He had become my confidant. If I cried, he would hold me. If I laughed, he would join me. If I needed to be silent, he wouldn't make a sound.

"I'm going," I shouted at the closed door.

He couldn't hear me. Tito Fuentes was back on full blast.

Lovely died on Saturday. My mother didn't find out until Sunday afternoon. Since my grandmother had died, and she had moved down with Uncle Shot three years ago, she gets touchy when others in her small town know things before she does. This seemed to be the main topic of discussion when she called to tell me about Lovely's death.

"Claudine, Tully, and Ms. Bernice all knew by dinnertime on Saturday," she said when she called. "I can't imagine why no one had the decency to tell me. They all know how close you and Lovely were as children. I've been fuming ever since. To think, I had to find out in Sunday service. I almost fell off the pew."

I switched the phone to my other ear.

"Mom, none of that really matters now, does it?"

"Well I guess it doesn't," she sighed.

"What happened to Lovely? Was she sick?"

Finally giving more weight to my questions than her hurt feelings, she answered me.

"Some kind of accident, Baby. I'm not sure. A few people say she may have even killed herself."

After she had said those words, a rhythmic thud echoed in my ears.

As she continued to go on and on about matters concerning her neighbors and the cliques she was not a part of, I pictured Lovely standing at the end of the road that led to my grandmother's house. It's where she waited at the start of each summer to greet me. Although I always begged Uncle Shot to stop so I could jump out of the car and into the sun to begin our welcome dance, my grandmother never allowed it.

"No need for that Cecely, she can walk on up to the house," my grandmother would say. "Look. She hasn't washed today more than any other day. You need some other friends around here. Lovely has the upbringing of a mule, and the sense to match."

I would turn around, digging my knees into the back seat of Uncle Shot's Buick and wave and holler as loud as I could.

"Lovely!"

Lovely would run behind the car paying no mind to the dust the billowed up to choke her.

"Sissy! You're here! You're here!"

My apartment was my sanctuary. Each piece of furniture selected over time, set in just the right place. Nothing had that mundane feel of matching décor. An antique straight back wooden chair here, a modern red blush chaise lounge there. Soft, flowing curtains dressed the windows. The paintings and photographs that hung on the walls all had history. Many of my belongings were transplants from my previous studio apartment. I had been clear-headed enough at that point in my life to ensure that nothing I brought to this space carried a hint of pain. Some friends disagreed with the choice to get rid of objects associated with the less-than-happy times in my life, but hey, they didn't have to live here.

I moved back into this building when my mother sold it to me five years earlier. The neighborhood was changing. Some would say for the better; others would not agree. I grew up in this house. Artie Johnson, who rented the first floor from my mother for many years, was my piano teacher. During the rough patches when she rented out the third floor, a host of tenants became my babysitters, wisdom-givers, and friends. There was no pain here for me, only vibrant memories of a loving childhood and my most recent years of adult life. So it only seemed natural that what I moved back with me should reflect that same image. I had made the right choice.

Just as I slipped my foot into a steaming bath of jasmine-scented bubbles, the phone rang. She didn't even give me a chance to say hello.

"Are you coming down Cecely?" My mother's voice was always quick, yet somehow gentle. I tried to situate myself in the tub before answering. "Well?" she asked again.

"Yes, Mom. I'll be there," I answered, sliding down into the warm water. "I'll let my principal know that I won't be able to join the summer school staff on opening week. But I can't stay long, Mom, just a few days."

She started in again on not being among the first to know about Lovely, and how Uncle Shot's nonchalant attitude toward her feelings bothered her. I tried to listen. I swear I did, but my thoughts drifted to memories of my old friend.

The first summer I traveled to the small town of Pineville, North Carolina, it was 1975 and I was ten years old. My grandmother had come to New York to be my escort. I had never been more than five miles from my home in Harlem. My boundaries included my house, school, the stores along the corner of my block, the intersecting streets, and, on occasion, church. The few friends I did have lived within that perimeter, and although I was not allowed to visit their homes, we played on their stoops.

The train ride south was mesmerizing. I took in each sight beyond the window's pane and attempted to record it in my memory.

When the porter's thundering voice announced the approaching stops, I would ready myself so as not to miss a glimpse of another city's train station. I would later tell my friends back home that I'd been to such and such a place, when in fact I had only passed through. My grandmother often warned me of the evils of stretching the truth. My Uncle Shot was just the opposite; he would praise me for using my imagination.

On this first trip, my grandmother, who was not known for being a patient woman, tired quickly of my youthful energy and tireless questions.

"When we gonna get there, Grandmom?" I asked.

"Soon enough."

I'd let the train roar on through a station or two and then could not contain myself.

"How many more stops?"

She gave me a stern look. "Don't worry me, girl. Shush and enjoy the ride."

Her admonition did not deflate my excitement. I pressed my face against the window even harder and watched as the big city buildings of the North slowly transformed into the cornfields and tobacco rows of the South.

As Uncle Shot drove us from the train station, and he and Grandmom discussed things that "only concerned grown folks," it suddenly hit me that they would be my only companions for the summer. I had no cousins. My mother packed four books for me to read. To most children that would have seemed like a chore, but reading was what my mother called "my forte." I wondered how long it would be before I ran out of pages to read. Just then, Uncle Shot turned the car off of the paved road and onto a dirt path.

"Here we are, Sissy," Uncle Shot said with a grin, looking at me over his shoulder. "You home now, Baby Girl."

"Watch out now, Shot!" Grandmom yelled. "There goes that silly child of Rose's." Sitting there on the ground by the edge of a freshly painted white fence was a girl.

"Go on now." Grandmom shouted out the window, waving

her hand as if shooing off a flock of birds or some other nuisance. "Go home to your own place."

Uncle Shot turned toward her and grimaced. "Ain't no sense in being so hard, Mama," he said. "She don't mean no harm. No harm at all."

With that, he continued up the road. I pulled myself up from the deep car seat, turned around, and peered through the window. The girl stood up and brushed off her legs. With one hand held above her eyes to block the sun's rays, she lifted her other hand high and waved at me.

Much later that evening when all the dishes had been washed and neatly placed in the cupboards, I asked Uncle Shot about the girl by the fence. He was sitting in an old chair on the enclosed porch off the kitchen, gazing through the rusted screen. This seemed to be his place of solitude, and I decided to make it mine too. It was by far the smallest room on the premises. The rest of the house was grander than I had expected. I spent the earlier part of the day discovering every inch of it. A large front porch wrapped around the house. Tall windows reached from the high ceilings down to the hardwood floors. Fine floral rugs were situated around the sitting room. The furniture was old but polished to a glossy shine. The stairway was wide and led to a spacious second floor hall with windows at opposite ends. This hall was larger than my bedroom at home. There were five spacious rooms, one across from the other in a zigzag pattern. My room was furthest from the stairs, but overlooked a glorious, sprawling open field covered with wildflowers and flooded with sunshine.

"Why do you smoke a pipe, Uncle Shot?" I asked interrupting the quiet. This was my way of starting the conversation.

"Why not?" he answered, motioning with his hand for me to sit down on the rocker next to him.

"It probably isn't so good for you. Don't you think?" I looked straight ahead through the screen to avoid his eye contact.

I didn't like tricking Uncle Shot much. He seemed to be very nice. I had only seen him two other times that I could remember. Both times were back home in New York, and they were brief.

"How old are you Sissy?"

From that I assumed our conversation about smoking was over. I corrected most people when they called me Sissy by spelling my name out slowly and harshly, "It's C-E-C-E-L-Y, Cecely, not Sissy." But I didn't correct my uncle. It sounded alright coming from him.

"I'm ten," I answered. "My birthday was June 10th. My mom gave me a party and everything."

I quickly took my chance to turn the conversation my way.

"I sure wish I had a friend or two to spend this summer with." I rocked the chair a bit faster.

"Don't get me wrong, I'm happy to be someplace different, but aren't you supposed to meet different people when you go different places?" I kept rocking, anxiously awaiting his reply.

"You know," Uncle Shot began, as he stood and walked closer to the screen. "You are just like your mama." Then he began to laugh hard and deep, his round belly jumping to the beat of his laughter.

"How so?" I asked walking over to join him.

He was a tall man. At least it seemed that way to me. The closest I ever stood to another man was Pastor Berry, but everyone remarked on how short he was. A "low rider" is what they called him, but not to his face, of course.

"Talk like her, too."

With this, he laughed even harder. I did, too. He patted the top of my head. "How so" was definitely one of my mother's sayings. Oh goodness! When did I start saying that?

Chacho didn't find it funny when he returned home the next day to find that I had borrowed his new set of luggage. While talking with him on the phone at the airport, I could picture vividly his every gesture as he all but cussed me out.

"This move in no way compares to that Raggedy Ann, powder blue sweat suit I confiscated from you! You planned to give that away.

You have lost your mind!"

"Cha—," I tried to squeeze in, but he continued.

"Don't you scratch it. And most of all, don't bring it back here with no country dust on it!"

"Chacho," I finally got a word in. "I'm not keeping it, I'm borrowing it. You were the one who encouraged me to go down there to pay my respects to Lovely, remember? And no respectable girl goes on a trip without the proper luggage."

I knew his face would be turning red at this point, but I also knew he would agree. "See ya!" With that I quickly hung up the phone.

As I approached my gate, I could hear the boarding call for my flight in the distance. "Now boarding flight 461 to Raleigh-Durham. All passengers needing assistance and families with small children will be boarding first."

As usual, everyone who was anything but a child, an elderly person, or someone needing assistance, mobbed the entrance to the boarding ramp. As I let out an impatient sigh, I was joined in my exasperation by a man standing next to me. I hadn't noticed him before.

"I know," the man leaned in and whispered. "Isn't it crazy? We all have tickets with assigned seats and people act like we're boarding a city bus."

Although I would have normally ignored a stranger's attempt at small talk, I returned his response with a thin smile. Shifting the strap of my carry-on to the other shoulder, I turned to face him and replied politely, "I was just thinking the same thing."

"My name is Ezra Morris," he said, his hand extended to greet me. I shifted my sweater to my left arm and reached out to acknowledge his introduction.

"Hello. I'm Cecely."

"Got a last name, Miss Cecely?"

"Um, it's Dodd. Cecely Dodd."

With this, I realized that I hadn't really taken the stranger in. Since I'd shared my full name, I became more aware of the need to assess the man I was speaking to. He looked alright for an older man. Not strikingly handsome, but nice looking. Tall and casually dressed.

Strong jaw, bright eyes. Brown skin. Sounded normal, but there was something a bit different—almost striking—about him. I figured him to be around my mother's age.

The attendant called for my seating group and I moved forward to join the other passengers. I could feel the older man behind me. I had to will myself not to turn around. By the time the plane landed, my pre-board conversation was a faint memory. I pulled out my phone to call the house and headed for the baggage claim area. I half hoped that my mother would answer, which would ensure that Uncle Shot and I would have the ride home alone. Mom and I could catch up later. I had a craving for some alone time with my uncle.

Uncle Shot walked into the kitchen on the second morning of that first summer in his home and casually brought up what I was afraid to ask about the day before.

"I guess you want to know what that little girl's name is, the one down by the fence yesterday." I didn't have a chance to answer, my mouth was so full, and I couldn't chew fast enough to get the food down. "Her name is 'Lovely'," he said walking toward the coffee pot to pour a cup.

"Lovely, huh? Let me get that for you Uncle Shot," I offered, making my way toward the stove.

"Go on girl," he replied stirring sugar into his cup. "Little girls like you should be playin' outside by this time of day. Your grandmother's at church already this mornin'. You ought to make the best of that. Go on."

I plopped back down in the chair and rested my chin in my hands. "Play with who?"

Uncle Shot gave me a curious look, raised his brow and pointed through the window toward the road. I pushed back from the table, and was halfway down the road before I heard the screen door slam shut behind me. A few pebbles quickly found their way into my sneakers and slowed me down. I bent down to take off my shoes and shake them out. When I stood up, there she was. Rumpled dress. Messy hair. Barefoot.

"You're pretty," she said. "What's your name?"

"Sissy," I answered smoothing my hair back with my hands. That was the first time I had ever introduced myself that way.

"I'm Lovely. I live down the road there, around the bend, behind them trees." She pointed with her arm fully extended. "My mama's name is Rose. It's really Rosalie, but everybody calls her Rose."

"Oh." I was shocked by all that information at once, but felt obliged to return the same. "My mom's name is Arlene."

"You a Cole? I'm a Fletcher. Lovely Rose Fletcher."

"No, I'm not a Cole. My grandmother is a Cole. I'm a Dodd."

"I don't know no Dodds."

I didn't know any Fletchers, but didn't think it mattered enough to say. Cole was my grandmother's last name. Taking the time to braid one side of her hair, she gave me a good once over. She scanned my yellow t-shirt and bright orange shorts and then looked into my eyes. Her eyes danced, and she then took in my skinny legs and sneakers. Back home in New York on the playground, some girls would have taken all this studying the wrong way, but I knew better. Her eyes told a different story.

I was thin compared to the girls in my school, and although Lovely was probably no thinner, she sure looked it. Her faded gray dress hung on her like a sack. It was old and worn, but not dirty. I couldn't say the same for her feet. My mother had told me that many children in Pineville played outside with no shoes and in the same breath told me, 'And you'd better not!'

We were silent for a few moments. She braided the other side of her hair and I shook more pebbles from my shoe. Then she began again.

"I bet we're the same age." She stepped in real close and swung her hand across the tops of our heads to measure our heights. "I'm gonna be eleven next month. My mama said I'm sure to have a party this year, but she says that every year."

She dropped her head and peeked up at me to see my reaction. I didn't know what the right reaction was until she burst out laughing. I sensed her relief and joined her.

Finally, we sat down under the big magnolia tree. The grass beneath it was soft and warm. It seemed out of place in contrast to the dusty dirt road beside it. We sat across from one another, legs folded Indian style, and got acquainted.

The number of things we had in common was surprising, and with the knowledge of each one, we giggled and hoped for more. We were the same age, lived alone with our mothers, never knew or could not remember our fathers, had no siblings, loved strawberry licorice, and hated boys. It wasn't more than a half hour before Grandmom pulled the car onto the road. She summoned me through the car window to get back to the house and help her make dinner. I knew she didn't need my help in the kitchen. So it was on my second day in Pineville that I sensed two important truths: my grandmother wanted to keep me away from Lovely, and I would do everything I could to stop her.

I called the house to let Uncle Shot know my plane had landed. No answer. I settled down in a hard chair near Baggage Claim and waited.

"Is someone coming to get you?"

It was Ezra Morris—the man I met at the gate.

"Yes," I replied, this time getting a better look at him. His frame was leaner than what would normally appeal to me. But why was I concerned about appeal? I hardly knew this man.

"Well, Miss Dodd," he said, stretching his hand toward me. "I have to be on my way. Pleased to have met you." I sat up in the chair and leaned forward to accept his hand. His grip was firm but gentle.

"Thank you," I replied. "I hope you have a nice stay." I expected a reply, but he smiled and walked toward the revolving door.

My plane hadn't been scheduled to arrive for another ten minutes, so I knew not to expect Uncle Shot right away. I sat back in the chair and my thoughts wandered back to a dream I'd had the night before.

There was Lovely, standing right up on my grandmother's porch. She looked to be about twenty-five. Through the years her body caught up with her baggy dresses, but in the dream, she was skinny again, almost sickly. Her face was sad and worn. Something was wrong. The Lovely I knew was always smiling. From the first year I met her to the last year I saw her. Five years in all. Because of this, I knew I was dreaming and tried to wake myself up. It didn't work.

Ms. Rose was there too, standing on the dirt road in front of the house. She had not aged a bit. She looked the same as the day I laid eyes on her. Blouse too tight, one hand on her hip, the other holding a Lucky Strike cigarette to her lips. She was saying, "Come on now, Lovely, you your mama's child. No sense in frettin' over small things. You gonna be alright just like me."

Now enough was enough. This had to be a dream. The only person my grandmother disliked more than Lovely was Ms. Rose. There's just no way she could be that close to Grandmom's porch. I realized that I was also in the dream, but I couldn't see myself.

"I don't understand why," Lovely said with such pain, it was more like a whimper. I could feel my whole body shudder. Then she wrapped her arms around her waist and squeezed real tight. She was hurting. I could feel myself walking toward her, but never made it close enough.

I was so lost in my recall of the dream that I didn't notice Uncle Shot had come through the revolving door.

"If I was a snake, I woulda bit you," Uncle Shot said as he drew closer.

"Oh, Uncle Shot. I'm sorry. I was lost in my thoughts." I looked down at my watch. "My plane just landed. You made good time." I looked at him feeling the same way I had always felt around him: warm and loved.

"Yeah Girl, good time, good time." He grabbed my bags and limped toward the revolving door. "Your mama's in the car."

It had been fifteen years since I had last seen him. Fifteen years since my grandmother had passed away. He didn't have a limp back then. It looked like the problem was at the top of his leg. His hip, I'd guess. I started to ask him and then decided not to. I thought of my first Ken doll. Tammy Thomas, a girl whose family once rented our third floor, snapped Ken's leg off and no matter what my mother tried to do to fix it, that leg never worked right again. To this day, Tammy lives in Harlem, and every time I see her, I still want to fight her.

The last time I had seen my mother was when she came back to visit me in New York three years ago. Not seeing your mom for three years is three years too long. Every school year since I had started teaching, I worked summers for extra money, which meant I wasn't making time to visit. As I approached the car, I could see her sitting in the front seat. I started to tear up. Gray hair covered her head, but she was still beautiful! As I got closer, she opened the car door and stepped onto the curb.

"Hey Baby," she said, while giving me a long warm hug. "It's been much too long."

I cupped her face in my hands and planted a kiss on her cheek. "Mom, you look marvelous!" We laughed through our tears, got in the car, and headed home.

I started to tell them about my dream and then decided to wait. After all, it was just a dream. All those years had passed, and I'd never dreamt of Lovely before. I thought of her fondly many times, but I'd never dreamt of her. I probably was more affected by her passing than I realized.

Grandmom's house was about forty-five minutes from the airport. We always called it Grandmom's house, even though she had gone to be with the Lord some time ago. On the way home, our conversation jumped around from my mother's concern with my love life to how "cliquish" she felt the people of Pineville had become. She had grown up here, left as a young woman, and returned. I kept telling her that people formed bonds over time and that it wasn't personal. Claudine Barrett Brown and Talutha Graham Green (Tully) were my mother's childhood friends. She moved north while they stayed in Pineville, pursuing their desire to marry into the "right kind" of family. Both of their mothers had been close friends with my grandmother for years, and also were instrumental in their daughters' choice of husbands.

Ms. Claudine married John Brown, who inherited the first black-owned funeral home in Pineville. Ms. Tully married Pastor Noah Green's son, Noah Green Jr., who succeeded his father as pastor of Greater Grace Baptist Church. Sometime during the many years my mother lived in New York, the two had befriended Bernice Mack. Ms. Bernice was Lovely's neighbor and from what I remember as a child, a very kind-hearted woman. Ms. Bernice had never married, and she was not originally from Pineville.

Pineville was and is like many small southern towns, full of gossip and ghosts. Although the surrounding towns were predominantly white, Pineville boasted of a mixture of the races. Blacks who once worked for whites no longer did. They now owned considerable acres of land, stores, and barbershops. It had been that way for years. The property and businesses were passed down through generations, and for the most part remained within the original families. Everyone knew everybody else's business, and dead issues were never laid to rest. As soon as someone's business, good or bad, made its way through the grapevine, you would hear things like, "Well you know his daddy was the same way," or "I knew eventually that dirt was going to catch up with her, remember when..."

There was hardly much talk of the future. There weren't enough hours in the day to talk about that. It was definitely the past and the present that dominated the early morning phone calls and late-night porch talks in Pineville.

The car rounded the bend and turned onto the dirt road. I looked out the back window as I had done year after year in anticipation of seeing Lovely. The old magnolia tree stood as tall as ever, casting an enormous circle of shade around the spot where we used to meet. Uncle Shot glanced at me in the rearview mirror and smiled softly. He understood that this place was special for me.

That first year of friendship was the hardest for Lovely and me. Not of our own doing, but because of my grandmother's opposition to it. Our meeting under the magnolia tree became a daily ritual. I would rush around the house completing every chore Grandmom had assigned to me. The chores weren't hard, just tedious—things she wrote on a slip of paper simply to keep me busy. I half-ate my breakfast, half-cleaned, and would have half-dressed if necessary, just to make it to that tree by ten o'clock.

Near our grand magnolia tree rested an old, sturdy cart without wheels. Beyond it was a creek where the water was shallow. It cascaded over the rocks and flowed under a small wooden bridge—the same bridge you had to cross to get to Lovely's house. The field between the cart and the creek was full of wildflowers, but here and there were places big enough for us to sit and hide. There, in our wonderland, we braided each other's hair, traded stories about the girls we hated at school, told our secrets, and read books. Well, I did all the reading in the beginning. Lovely said her eyes were bad and that she didn't want to strain them. Plus, she said she liked the way I read. So I did. I read out loud and changed my voice for every character. After we would read a particular story a few times, Lovely would know the words by heart and mouth them along with me. It wasn't until our second summer together that I realized she couldn't read. She told me jokes she heard from the men who frequented her house. Some were funny, and others I would be ashamed to repeat even now. I taught her dance steps to all the newest songs. I would sing them over and over until she knew all the words and we would put on a show for the wildflowers.

Lovely taught me about people, perhaps unintentionally, but she did. She would just be talking about this thing or that, sharing her thoughts about why so and so did such and such a thing and I'd listen. She knew way more adults than I did. Back home in New York, the only adults I knew were teachers, a storekeeper or two, the pastor of our church, my Sunday school teacher and one or two of my mother's tenants. But I never heard the kind of things that passed by Lovely's ears.

Uncle Shot glanced at me through the rear-view mirror once more.

"Yeah," he said softly, "I still look for Lovely to be standing there, too. She sure was a precious girl, right precious."

That is what he always said about her, even to my grandmother. Every time she came home from running errands, or attending a committee meeting, or visiting a sister from church, she would either ride up beside Lovely and me at the magnolia, or shout my name as loud as thunder from the porch. Whichever method she chose, her intent was to break up our play time or as she called it, "to put an end to our daydreaming."

It never failed. As soon as I swung open the screen door, from whatever room in the house she occupied, I could hear her.

"I guess you thought you were gonna kick up the dust with that child all day, huh? Don't you have anything better to do? If not, I'll find something for you. Yes, I will."

She made a different remark each time, but they all meant the same thing: I don't like Lovely.

My mother didn't join in when Uncle Shot and I reminisced about my summers in Pineville. She never knew the young Lovely— Lovely the child, Lovely my friend. Her impression had been formed by the town gossip and my grandmother's venomous words. Popular opinion was that Lovely was "touched," "the daughter of a drunken floozy,"

"Rose's chile."

When I returned home each September, as my mother unpacked my suitcase and neatly placed clean clothes back into drawers, I'd gush with information and tales of my adventures with Lovely. My mother never took much interest in my stories of those summers, but it didn't matter to me.

"We ate some of them sour apples nobody likes, and they weren't as bad as you said." My excitement showing, I couldn't stand still, pacing the floor and bouncing on the side of the bed. She would just smile as if preoccupied with her own thoughts. Can't she hear me? Doesn't she see what a great friend I've found?

"Grandmom doesn't like Lovely or Ms. Rose, but they're nice people, Mom. Maybe not the kind of people Grandmom is used to. They're not church-going people, but everybody who goes to church isn't so nice either. Even you say that."

I looked for her reaction, a small affirmation that I was right and my grandmother was wrong. Nothing.

"I met a boy and he—"

Now I had her attention! She gave me a harsh look and then we smiled, knowing I was only playing. And that would be that. After she left my room and I settled back into my surroundings, I'd replay the summer over and over in my mind. I'd laugh out loud just thinking of something Lovely had said or we had done. The memories were so good, that they would entertain me until Christmas came.

After I had a chance to freshen up from the flight and gorge myself on hearty helpings of my mother's barbecue, collards, cornbread, and banana pudding, we sat around the kitchen table shooting the breeze. Try as we might to remain upbeat, the topic often turned back to Lovely.

"Terrible thing that somethin' like that would happen to somebody's child," Uncle Shot said, stuffing his pipe with tobacco and shaking his head real low. "Precious girl. I hope they get to the bottom of what really happened. Precious girl like that, I mean right precious."

"That's not how most people remember her, Shot," my mother rebuffed her brother. She adjusted a crooked napkin in the holder at the center of the table.

Uncle Shot looked up from his pipe, chin still pointed to his chest, eyes peering over his glasses, and focused intently on her.

"Well Arlene, that's how I remember her. You would think the folks in this town would have business of their own to tend to. Worried too much 'bout the next person, I think. So busy looking for the splinter in their neighbor's eye that they can't see the two-by-four in their own. Shoot, they had just about as much to say about you when you left for New York. You remember that don't you? Sure, you remember."

He got up and headed towards the porch. My mother got up real slow and brushed some imaginary crumbs off the front of her apron.

"I don't recall any such thing, Shot. And even if they were talking, they weren't saying the same things."

She was trying to remain calm, but I could see her feathers were ruffled.

Uncle Shot walked onto the porch, but his voice carried. "We weren't talking about what you recalled. I asked you to remember."

"What's he talking about, Mom?"

She swallowed hard and hurried over to the sink as if trying to find a use for her hands. A section of hair had loosened from her bun and brushed across her eye. It wasn't just me who was affected by Lovely's death. Everybody seemed frazzled. As I was about to get up, in walked Uncle Shot, his lit pipe in hand.

"Listen Sissy, it's your mother's place to speak for herself. I was out of line. After all these years I must be allowing these nosy folks to rub off on me."

He was waving away the smoke with his hand, knowing full well no one ever smoked in my grandmother's house.

"But I will say one thing that's worth the words," he continued. "Your grandmother and the rest of this stone-throwing town moved all their hate from Rose Fletcher right onto her daughter's back, as soon as she got grown. Lovely ain't to blame for her mother's sins no more than I am for mine or you is for yours. And that's a fact."

Poor Uncle Shot. I knew his intention was to offer my mother a sideways apology, yet instead he piqued my interest even more. I stared at him, wondering if he would try to redeem himself. Then he walked through the porch and out to the yard. I turned to look at my mother, but she had left the room.

"Your mama drink shine?" Lovely asked as she parted my hair down the middle.

I knew it wasn't a casual question. How could it be? Every question she asked was linked to something or another. If she asked one, she really wanted to know, and eventually you'd find out why.

"Don't be shame," she continued, tugging at my hair as she braided it. "I ain't gonna tell nobody."

I had no idea what shine was, but I figured it must be bad if someone would be ashamed of drinking it. We were sitting on the back of the cart, swinging our bare feet in the early evening light. My shoes lay in the grass, and although I had taken up the habit of playing in my bare feet, my grandmother could never know it. I never answered Lovely's question that day. Somehow the subject changed, the sun fell, and before I knew it, I was in the house getting ready for bed.

"You need to go down to the church with me some mornings, Sissy," my grandmother said one night during my second summer in Pineville. "It would be good for you to help me when I visit the sick or help the pastor's wife prepare the church for weekly service."

I sat down between her legs as she combed my hair, creating a style that Lovely would only undo the next day.

"Your mother should be doing your hair." She tugged. "Girls your age still need their mother's hands in their heads." I knew there was more to what she was saying. And then it came.

"The girls down at the church are very nice. They are growing up into wonderful young ladies. Learning manners and serving on committees as young as twelve years old. You'll meet plenty of friends down there."

"Can Lovely come?" I asked, wincing from the tightness of her braiding.

"Well that's my point, Cecely. Lovely is a bit too common for me, and you too, for that matter. Can't you see that she doesn't wash well? Whenever I see her, she is wearing that same dingy dress."

I tilted my head back and looked up into my grandmother's eyes. Her complexion was flawless. She was beautiful just like my mother. I could only hope to be that pretty someday. I could smell the sweet cherry blossom perfume she always wore. Her lipstick was dark pink, her teeth were straight and shiny, not crooked like my bottom ones. The hands that braided my hair were perfectly manicured.

"Why don't you like Lovely, Grandmom? If she wears the same two or three dresses every day, I don't see how that could be her fault." She pushed my head forward so that I was looking straight ahead again. It seemed that she was braiding even tighter now, but I couldn't end it there.

"She's my friend," I whispered.

She finished the last row, put the top back on the jar of hair grease and nudged me with her knee to let me know she was done.

"Well you could do better," she said, walking toward my bedroom door. "Dirt rubs off, you know. In more ways than one. As far as I can see, she's headed in the same direction as her loose mother. Always talking and staring with them Fletcher eyes. All those Fletchers got eyes that shine bright with mischief."

I didn't want to seem as if I was sassing my grandmother. My mother would tear my behind up good even at the thought of it, so I didn't defend Lovely anymore that night. My mother reminded me to be sure to attend church on Sundays like we did together back in New York, and I had. Going there to get new friends wasn't on my agenda. Lovely was all the friend I needed.

During that summer, Lovely brought up the subject again.

"My mama drinks shine," she announced while we were catching fireflies. "She drinks it a lot. Too much, I suspect. Sometimes she goes down to Wally's to get groceries for supper but don't come back with nothing but a jar of shine and a grin."

I realized shine must be whiskey. Lovely hopped up on the cart and opened her jar to put in a few blades of grass.

"It's okay though," she said sheepishly, holding up the jar to see if the insects would eat the grass. "Ms. Bernice always sends over two plates when mama gets like that. I'm not sure how she know mama done got her hands on some shine, but them plates sure is good and they come right on time."

I caught two fireflies and transferred one to Lovely's hand. We put them in our jars and then smelled our sweaty palms.

"Pee-yew!" we shouted together, and then fell out laughing on the ground.

We said our goodnights and as she walked down the road toward her house, I finally gave her the long-awaited answer.

"Lovely," I called, and she turned around to wave again. "No, my mama don't drink shine."

Sometimes Lovely would wear the same unwashed dress for days, but she was my wondrous, beautiful friend, and I didn't want another one. I often wanted to share my clothes with her. Each year my mother packed seven pairs of shorts and a shirt to match each one. When I thought I could get away with it, I would hide a real dirty set from my grandmother and wear it outside later that week.

Lovely would have the nerve to say, "What you got that dirty old set on for? You better change quick before we do our steps for the wildflowers. You gonna embarrass me!"

Sometimes I would run back in and change. This all depended on my grandmother's whereabouts at the time. Lovely knew Grandmom would tie fire to my butt if I got caught. She also knew I was doing it for her.

I didn't feel comfortable going to my mother right after Uncle Shot's hint about some family secret, so I decided to make it an early night and went to bed. The funeral was in just a few days and the thought of drama wore heavy on my mind. Before I knew it, I was out like a light, and then there she was again.

> She was standing at my grandmother's front door holding her hand up as if ready to grab hold of the knocker. Ms. Rose was standing behind her off to the side. I was there again, and Lovely kept looking back at me down on the lawn.
>
> "Don't do it girl. Ain't nothing gone change," Ms. Rose said between cigarette drags. Lovely hesitated. She looked at the door and then back at me.
>
> "Sissy, I want to know, don't you?"
>
> I didn't know what was going on. Know what? I wanted to ask her what she meant. I opened my mouth but nothing came out.
>
> Ms. Rose flicked her cigarette butt into the grass and folded her arms across her chest. "If she's right, you'll want to know."
>
> Lovely was a grown woman, a young woman, but grown nonetheless. Her dress was tighter and fit her awkwardly. Ms. Rose threw her head back and laughed—hard and ugly. Then Lovely slammed the knocker down hard one time.
>
> "I have to, Sissy," she said. "It's only right. Right as rain."

I awoke with a jolt, the dream replaying in my mind. I needed to know what Lovely meant. What was "only right"? What would I want to know?

I decided to give Chacho a call. I was happy to have someone to talk to about everything that was going on. I described my dreams in detail and he listened without interruption. I expressed my angst about having these dreams after all these years. Since I'd never shared my history with Lovely before tonight, Chacho asked a lot of questions and I was forced to remember events that now held more significance to me. I didn't believe there was a connection between the secrets implied by Uncle Shot and the ghost of my friend, but figured I'd talk about it since Chacho was a listening ear.

After I was finished, and he sensed it was safe, he interjected.

"Is her mother still around? What's her name, Rosie? Maybe talking with her will ease your heart some. The dreams are probably natural. Someone who was dear to you passed away."

"You know, you're right. I should stop by to give her my condolences before the funeral," I said feeling a bit better. "And her name is Rose," I laughed. "Not Rosie."

"Same thing," he said breathing deeply and way too loudly. "Now that I've missed my favorite television shows attending to your drama, let's get down to my business. How soon after the funeral are you coming back to New York?"

"I'm not sure. Are you watering my plants?"

"Here we go," he started. "Let's get four things straight, Southern Belle. I'm busy, I'm busy, and I'm busy. You tying me up with these chores is a burden to my lifestyle. Get your head and your heart straight and get back here soon."

"Chacho," I whispered. I knew his nice side would wear off eventually. "I have a new CD on my bedroom dresser. If I'm not mistaken, it's one of your favorite artists. It's yours for being a dear and helping me out."

"Oh, that old thing? I've been playing it all day."

"Boy, I'm gonna hurt you," I shouted, quickly covering my mouth so as not to disturb the house. We were both laughing now.

"Alright, I'll do these cumbersome chores, but you owe me, and you will pay."

"Thanks, Chacho. By the way, you said you had four things to say and only gave me three. What's the fourth?"

"Well, I'm doing everything in fours lately. I saw a palm reader today and—"

"Chacho, I can't believe you!"

"Listen. I saw a palm reader today and she told me that if I was in the business of straightening folks out, which I am, then for the next few days I should leave them all with four things."

"So, what's my fourth one?" I asked, feeling like a glutton for punishment.

"I miss you," he said softly, and with that, he hung up the phone.

✺

When the sun forced its way through the blinds, I decided to get up and go see Ms. Rose. The aroma of a true southern breakfast reached the second floor and made its way under my door. My mother was a good cook, but I knew it was Uncle Shot stirring up all the things that would have me in the gym on overtime when I got back home. I made my way to the kitchen and saw him at the table with a cup of hot coffee. My mother was nowhere in sight, so I figured she went out.

"You wouldn't believe how much like your mama you've come to be," Uncle Shot said as he set a heaping plate of food on the place-mat in front of me. "Eat up. Seems you could use this here plate and maybe a second one. You just about a string bean, if you ask me. Ain't they serving food in New York?"

"Where'd Mother go?" I asked, separating my eggs from every-thing else on the plate as I always did. "I know she's not with Tully and her bunch after all that talk yesterday."

"Of course, she is. Where else would she be? They believe that Rose ain't got the good sense to put her daughter away proper, so they intend to lead the planning. Now ain't that something? Tully and Claudine ain't been to Rose's house ever, and I mean ever, but they gonna strut over there like they been friends for life. Your mama ain't much better, but I'm not the one to tell her. At least she's got sense enough not to darken Rose's doorstep after all these years. She went up to the church to help with other things. Your mama ain't spoke to Rosalie Fletcher since she moved back down here."

We sat and enjoyed our breakfast together. He asked me how I was handling Lovely's passing, and I told him that it helped talking things through the night before with Chacho. I explained that he used to be a tenant but now was a great friend. I talked to Uncle Shot about Chacho much the same way we talked about Lovely all those years ago. I didn't dare bring up the things he had hinted at last evening about my mother's past.

Uncle Shot watched me eat and listened as I described my eccentric friend and our relationship. When I was finished, he took the empty plate from in front of me and smiled.

"You may have lost a few pounds, but your soul has not changed one bit. It don't take a rocket scientist to know that what you got going with this Chacho fella ain't too far removed from what you had with Lovely. I got work to do out back, so I can't explain it all to you, and don't believe I would anyway, but you think hard about what I'm sayin'. You'll see I'm right. Right as rain."

I looked at him from behind as he filled the sink with water. "Right as rain," I thought. Isn't that what Lovely said in my dream? "Right as rain"? I walked over and kissed him lightly on the cheek, took the dish towel away and finished up the rest of the dishes. He made the breakfast. It was the least I could do, and besides, I couldn't go see Ms. Rose until Moe, Larry, and Curly were finished over there.

It wasn't until the end of my third summer in Pineville that I met Ms. Rose. My grandmother only allowed me to play with Lovely where we were within earshot and a quick eyeball from the house. It was late August, and Lovely was about to begin her school year. I was scheduled to catch the train back home by myself. Once again, I was nervous about the ride home alone, but Lovely managed to somehow make it alright.

"Remember Pippi Longstocking from that book we read and how she loved adventure? Just pretend you're her, and I bet it'll be great!"

Lovely said this with such excitement that she had convinced me. For someone who had never stepped foot out of Pineville, she had dreams beyond this world that she knew too well. She got real close as if to knock me over and said, "I'll be waiting to hear how everything went, so write it down and don't leave nothin' out. By the time we meet again, we'll be a whole year older, and who knows what new things will happen then?"

On the morning of the day I was to catch the train home, my grandmother went to pick up a cake from Tully that she wanted me to take back to my mother, and Uncle Shot took advantage of the time to allow the unimaginable.

"Before Lovely gets the chance to say her goodbyes, why don't you surprise her first?" He looked me in the eye.

I took off running down the dirt road that I had grown to love, rounded the corner, and flew across the small bridge, where behind a grove of pine trees was the most beautiful row of dogwoods I'd ever seen. My eyes were focused on these magnificent natural wonders and I wished I had walked this path in early spring to watch them bloom. Uncle Shot had showed me a Polaroid picture of one lone dogwood in spring's full bloom. It sat out behind the house when he was younger. He thought it a "beautiful sight," and so did I. The wildflowers we played among did not grow on this side of the creek. Maybe because of the lack of sunshine. I couldn't help but notice that although the sun hung in the same place in the sky, it was much darker and grayer over here. Two small houses sat back from the road that branched from a deeply rutted dirt path. I was bushed, and my heart was pounding hard. I finally slowed down to take in this place, a place that had been hidden from my sight these last three years.

I approached the smaller of the two houses knowing it was Lovely's because she told me that Ms. Bernice's was bigger than hers. The wood on the first step of the porch was split down the middle. The rest of the porch cried out in need of painting. I ran my hand around a post, looking closely trying to determine what color it might have been. The house sat at a slant as if it had been forced that way by a hard, west wind.

There was no screen door, and the front door hung crooked on the hinges. Dull, blue lace curtains draped outside of the open front windows and lay in empty flower boxes. I walked across the frail floorboards to peek around the side and almost fell through the rail when it gave way. I heard a thump and then fast-moving footsteps to the door.

"Well, well, you got to be little Miss Sissy."

Her voice startled me as I balanced myself on one foot trying to keep from falling into a bed of dead flowers.

"Yes, I'm Sissy. Are you Lovely's mother? I mean, Ms. Rose?"

I wiped my hands on the front of my shorts. I tried to act like the dirt wasn't there and asked if I could see Lovely.
Ms. Rose leaned back into the doorway, her two feet firmly planted on the porch.

"Lovely, little Miss Sissy is here."

She turned her attention back to me, and I suddenly felt unwelcome.

"You look a whole lot like your mama, but I guess you know that."

I shook my head in agreement. My hands began to sweat, and I tried to peek around her to see if Lovely was coming.

"I ain't seen hide nor hair of you all these summers. Was wonderin' when you'd find your way 'cross that bridge."

I knew to tell her the real reason why wasn't the right thing to say, so I just smiled.

"Have a seat. She comin'. Just wasn't expectin' you."

I sat down in a tired-looking rocker. The backs of my thighs began to sweat. Ms. Rose joined me, sitting on a ragged, plaid lounge chair.

"Lovely tells me you and her been readin' over there in them wildflowers."

I grinned again.

"I laid in them flowers before." She winked her eye and ran her hands back over her neatly arranged finger waves. "Never once to read though." She winked at me again.

She reached over to a small rusted table next to her, picked up a cigarette and lit it. She blew the smoke out hard. I wished Lovely would hurry up. My grandmother would be back soon, and Ms. Rose made my stomach hurt.

Her skin was yellow—lighter than Lovely's. Lighter than I imagined she'd be. She wasn't bright yellow like Lorraine Simmons from my math class, though. She and Lovely favored one another for sure, and her neck was long and lean like my mother's. I guessed all mothers had long lean necks. She wasn't at all like I had pictured her. She wore too much make up and her fingernails were painted nice. Toenails, too. Her dress clung closely to her thin frame, swimming in vibrant summer colors. The waves in her hair showed bright and lay neatly against her head. When Lovely came running out the slanted house, I almost expected her to be in a flowery dress, too.

"Sissy, oooh girl, you gonna get it. I'd better walk you back around to your grandma's."

She saw my eyes were still wandering all over her mother, and she adjusted her dingy dress on her shoulders.

"Come on. Sorry, Mama, we gotta go."

She yanked me by the wrist and practically snatched me off the porch. We walked down the path with Lovely pulling me all the way. I looked back at Ms. Rose standing there watching us go. The differences between her and Lovely were painfully apparent. It began with the way their hair was done and moved to the way they dressed. Even though Ms. Rose looked fancier on the outside, her eyes didn't shine the same as Lovely's, her mouth didn't curl up on one side when she smiled, and her voice didn't sound smooth and gentle like the creek at sunset. I heard Lovely tell me many times how much she was like her mama, but I didn't see it. Her mother was as good-looking a woman as

Lovely was a girl, but only on the outside. Something bad from deep inside Ms. Rose seemed to seep through to the outside, and it made me uneasy.

It was getting late, and I'd spent most of the day resting and looking through my grandmother's things in the back room. A few times I would remember something about her and laugh. The next time, a memory would come and I'd cry. I knew in my heart my grandmother loved me, and I believe I loved her back just as hard until I met Lovely. It wasn't until I met Lovely that I saw a side of my grandmother that I didn't know existed. That's what I meant about how Lovely taught me about people without realizing that she had.

Since Uncle Shot said my mother would never go to Ms. Rose's, and I was sure the church ladies didn't really care enough about her to stay too long, I made my way down the road and across the bridge. The dogwoods were still in their splendor, blooms spread full and wide. White clouds perched atop treetops like cotton candy. I almost tripped over my own feet once or twice while taking in the scenery. I finally collected myself and realized I had approached Ms. Rose's porch sooner than I thought. I guess as a child, things seemed farther away. The house was a corner store trip for me. The way my grandmother warned about it, you would have thought it was across town.

Two cars were parked on the side of the house. One was still running. I peeked into the idling car and saw a blue suitcase on the back seat. Then, without warning, there she was, Ms. Rosalie Fletcher. She was drunk. Time had not been her friend. Her face was worn and haggard. Her hair no longer had that silky shine. It was all just combed back straight, dry, undone. At first, I chalked it up to her being in mourning over Lovely, but upon closer inspection I realized she had grown into this look. Suddenly I was ten years old all over again. My heart started pounding, my hands grew clammy, and my stomach hurt. It seemed we were both caught off guard this time. Our eyes met but neither of our mouths opened. As I was about to greet her properly, a man stepped out of the house. I couldn't focus on his face because the sun blinded me. I lifted up my hand to shield the bright rays and there he was, plain as day. He brushed past Ms. Rose and walked in my direction.

"Miss Dodd," he said, making his way off of the porch.

The caved-in porch step was no longer there, and he had to jump to avoid falling. The sound he made when his feet hit the ground jolted his name back into my memory. Ezra Morris. He walked over and took my hand. I was limp. My arm would not even extend itself.

"So, we cross paths again. You know Rosalie?" He wore jeans and a blue button-down shirt.

"I knew Lovely. Well I guess you could say Ms. Rose too, but only through Lovely."

I found myself wishing that I had taken more care getting dressed. The man was twenty years my senior, yet something drew me to him. I had on a sweat suit and a baseball cap. I had never expected this.

"Lovely was family," he said. "I have to get back home right after the funeral and—"

"Oh, so y'all was family, huh?" Ms. Rose shouted, holding onto the wood rail and lowering each foot to the ground. "Don't act like I'm not here, Ezra. I'm the grievin' mother here. You two just stoppin' through."

Ezra walked back over and helped her to sit on the edge of the porch.

"I apologize, Rosalie. Your visitor took me by surprise. We're acquaintances from New York." With that, he patted her on the shoulder and headed toward the idling car.

"It was a pleasure seeing you again, Miss Dodd. Sorry for the loss of your friend." His eyes were watery. It showed me he meant what he had said.

"A pleasure?" Ms. Rose continued. "Ain't pleasure how all this got started in the first place?" She tried to pull herself up from the porch floor and fell.

Ezra approached me. This time his voice was low and soft.

"Listen, I'm sorry you had to hear this. Rose is taking this hard. I'm staying at my sister's house just a mile or so from here. Maybe we could get together and talk after the funeral. Could we do that?"

Ms. Rose got to her feet.

"Whisperin' led to some of this too. Ain't nothin' y'all two sayin' ain't passed these ears before." Her shrill voice turned into a choking cough, and I went to her aid.

"I'll see you in a few days," Ezra shouted from the open car window. Then he was gone.

Because Ms. Rose couldn't stand well, I took a seat next to her on the porch.

I was closer to Lovely's mother than I had ever been. For a moment I saw Lovely in her. Somewhere behind those bloodshot eyes and extra mascara. She lifted her head, tilted it to one side and looked at me real hard. Suddenly she burst out laughing. Tears began to roll down her face. I could actually feel the heat of the liquor as it escaped her throat and penetrated my nostrils.

"Ms. Rose, do you remember me?"

She wiped slobber from her mouth with her sleeve. "Depends on if you worth rememberin'."

"I'm Sissy, Freddie Cole's granddaughter from New York."

"Mrs. Freddie Cole. Well, that's a name I thought I wouldn't have to hear no more. You come to make my day worse, cause that's all Freddie Cole ever done for me."

I didn't know how to respond, but my stomach was calm now, so I decided to continue.

"I'm not here to make things more difficult for you. Lovely and I were friends, and I want to know what happened to her."

She grabbed hold of the rail and hoisted herself from her seat.

"Well," she breathed out, managing to turn herself around to face the house.

"If you ain't here to hurt me, how 'bout getting me to my couch and maybe then we'll see what you're really here for."

The inside of the house was not how I pictured it. I had crossed the bridge to this side of the creek against my grandmother's wishes a few times in the years I visited, but never once had I dared to go into Rosalie Fletcher's home. I helped her to the couch that matched the chair I sat in. The place wasn't fancy or well lit, but it was cozy. From my vantage point I could see the kitchen over to the right and it was in the same state. A Formica top table and four red padded chairs sat dead center, surrounded by a modest refrigerator, stove, sink and counter. There were a few casserole-type dishes spread on the table, evidence that Claudine, Tully, and Ms. Bernice had been there.

Ms. Rose laid her head on the back of the couch and closed her eyes. We sat in silence for what seemed like an hour before I mustered up the courage to begin again.

"Ms. Rose, what happened to Lovely? I mean what were the circumstances surrounding her passing?"

She replied so quickly it startled me. Eyes still closed. Head leaned back and swaying from side to side in the rhythm of her words.

"You the first one who said it correctly. What was the circumstances surrounding my chile's death? "Cause there was a lot of stuff surrounding it, you know?"

Her voice got raspier with each word and was followed by another coughing spell. She reached over to the small table next to her for a cigarette and lit it.

"I knew who you was soon as I stepped out onto the porch. Ezra thought he had me frazzled, but it take more than a Morris to wear out an old pro like myself. You wasn't just Lovely's friend way back then," she continued, blowing smoke toward the ceiling. "You was her only friend. And that's why I remember you. Not 'cause you just so happen to be Freddie Cole's granddaughter or Arlene's chile for that matter. Don't get me wrong, being those things is highly thought of by some folk 'round here. Just not by me."

I stood up and walked toward the middle of the room. "If you don't mind me in your kitchen, I could make you some coffee or maybe heat you up something to eat." I knew there was no love lost between my grandmother and Ms. Rose, but her mentioning my mother threw me off a bit.

"No," she answered, opening her eyes for the first time. She looked directly at me now. "The church of the Secret Sinners Society been here and left that food. I don't plan on eatin' none of it." She sat up. "They ain't never cared about me or my chile. Laid my sins on the table and made her pay my dues. They got dues to pay, too. Everybody thinks all that past, my past, your mama's past, Ezra's past is gonna be buried with my baby, but it ain't so." Her voice began to harden.

"The Coles and the Morrises helped destroy many a life down through the years. It wasn't until Lovely that it turned to death." Her eyes got wild, and she leaned forward across her lap, legs spread much too wide to be wearing a dress and said real slow, "Get out of my house."

I didn't hesitate. I got up and walked out the door. Maybe I was wrong to have come asking questions of a grieving mother. What made me think I had a right to? Because Lovely was my friend for five summers during my childhood?

The next two days were uneventful. I didn't feel or sleep well. My dreams were foggy. Whatever connection I had to Lovely in those slumbering hours was somehow gone. My mind was going in circles trying to figure out what Ms. Rose was talking about. I wanted to ask my mother or Uncle Shot but didn't want to bother them with the rants of a drunken woman. The night before the funeral I found a local newspaper near my mother's chair and read the headline of a news brief concerning Lovely's death. It read:

Young black woman found dead in Newcomb's Stream

Stream? In our stream, the one that ran under the bridge? The article was matter of fact—a total of three sentences. I began to feel sick again and laid down until morning.

I awoke the day of the funeral and knew I would need all the time I could get to gather myself. By nine o'clock I was ready.

Uncle Shot was working under the hood of his car, and my mother was scurrying between her bedroom and the bathroom readying herself. She seemed anxious or nervous. My mother had met Lovely only once when we were younger during one of the last summers I spent with her. Ms. Colette, my mother's best friend in New York, drove her to pick me up that day in late August. They hadn't planned to spend the night. Ms. Colette had to get back home to her husband and children. We were ready to go, and I begged to have a few more minutes to run over to Lovely's.

We stood on Lovely's porch hugging, crying, and reminiscing about the previous few weeks. The night before I took a bottle of my grandmother's perfume from her vanity. She had so many, and this one was more than half gone. My hope was that she would never miss it. I knew Lovely would treasure it more because it had one of those fancy white rubber squeeze pumps with the hanging gold tassel. I had just given it to her when I spotted my mother more than halfway up the road to the house.

"Cecely, come on now. Say goodbye to your friend. We have to get going. You know Ms. Colette has to..."

She never made it all the way to the house. Lovely jumped off the porch, disregarding the steps, and ran over to greet her. Before my mother realized what was happening, Lovely grabbed her hand.

"Hey Mrs. Dodd," she said trying to adjust her braids with one hand and smooth her dress with the other. "It's nice to finally lay eyes on you. Sissy loves you a lot, not more than I love my mama, but a lot. And oh boy, can she read!"

The look on my mother's face is engraved in my memory. She didn't expect the Lovely I spoke so much about, this fifteen-year-old girl, to have the mannerisms and nature of a child. Lovely ignored her odd expression and went on to tell her what good friends we were—

well actually more like sisters—blood sisters. I ran up to join them. I had to step in. Not to rescue the awkward moment, but because there were just some things my mother didn't need to know. If my mother had learned that we pricked our fingers with a sewing needle and mixed our blood together, she would tie fire to my backside. I could feel the warmth on my behind then and there.

"Well, it's nice to meet you too, Lovely," my mother managed to say when Lovely took a moment to pause. I stepped in between them.

"I'm coming mom. Go ahead. I'll be right there. I promise."

My mother hesitated for a minute, taking Lovely in one more time. She couldn't hide the amazement on her face. Finally, she turned to go, and Lovely and I hugged each other until it hurt. It was the last time I saw her.

"Alright, ladies," Uncle Shot hollered from the front yard. "Taxi's ready!"

My mother walked out into the living room. She was wearing the same black dress she wore to her mother's funeral. The hat was different, though. This time she wore one of her own, not my grand-mother's. I originally thought a hat would be appropriate for me as well, but after trying on nine or ten of them that morning, I realized I just wasn't old enough to pull it off.

Uncle Shot sat in the driver's seat waiting patiently, fac-ing straight forward. I stood on the porch while my mother put a few last-minute things into her purse. As I watched the road in the distance, I could see the cars pass by. Many more than usual. They had to be headed for the church. I couldn't help but wonder if those cars held hearts of hatred, love, or just a bunch of nosy Pineville people.

The funeral was simple, with little emotion from those who attended. It was as though the mourners were only there to see how Ms. Rose would lay her child out. Neither Lovely nor Ms. Rose were church members. Tully had asked her husband, Pastor Noah, to hold the service there as a favor to her. She felt it was the Christian thing to do. I was somewhat glad that my grandmother had preceded Lovely in death. She would have attended in full funeral regalia, black dress, black hat, black shoes, and black stockings. She would have sat close to the front, opposite the family and sniffled into a starched handkerchief. She would have attended out of Christian obligation and not out of sympathy for the bereaved family. I sat motionless throughout the service, occasionally staring blankly at the poorly crafted program in my hand. I could see Ms. Rose from the back as she leaned over into the chest of the man next to her and wept for her child. The man was Ezra Morris.

The funeral director, Claudine's husband, John Brown, announced the final viewing and I watched the faces and emotions of those who lined the aisles to view my very best friend. I heard from my mother that Claudine's husband could not be persuaded to handle a funeral that he wouldn't make any money off of, no matter how Christian it might be.

After Ms. Rose and Ezra Morris, my mother went through the procession with Ms. Bernice and Tully. They were followed by a few more familiar faces: Eggy Lee Pollard and his wife from the grocery store, Mrs. Hinton from the dress shop, and four-eyed Leroy Harper who was infatuated with Lovely in junior high.

I straightened up in the pew, and Uncle Shot gently touched my shoulder as an indication that he would escort me, and he did. My heart felt thick, my chest full and vision was blurred by tears. Somehow, I managed to drag my feet toward the front of the church. I looked toward Ms. Rose, and our weeping eyes met.

Lovely was beautiful. She always had been. Although I was the one adorned in bright summer sets and hair ribbons each summer, she was the real thing. Tattered dresses and uncombed hair could not overshadow a beauty like hers. The warmth and realness of her heart seeped through to her skin. Even in death she possessed something special that I knew I never had.

There is something magical about a love that is not born of expectation. I knew my mother, my uncle, and even my seditty grandmother loved me as a child. But that was expected. They were family. I was their blood. Lovely loved me for other reasons, and I reciprocated as best I could. Our first summer together seemed like an eternity as we learned about each other's lives, and shared thoughts and feelings. The next four summers flew by. We were growing up, and there were always new things to share. Secrets about boys we had crushes on, stories about our first periods, and shared longings for the fathers we never knew.

 I reached down to touch her cold hand, and like a raging flood once held back by a dam, my pain burst open. Tears ran from my soul. Every smile, every word, every dance we ever performed for the wild-flowers. My entire body shook as I wailed. I wrapped my arms as tightly as I could around my stomach and bent in that same place that hurt each time I saw Ms. Rose. I had not spoken to Lovely in more than fifteen years. I wrote letters. She wrote back maybe once or twice. I stopped going to my grandmother's the summer I turned sixteen. My life had begun to change. I met new friends at school. I discovered boys, joined choirs, track teams. In that moment it struck me like a bolt of lightning. Had Lovely's world changed as well, or did time just stand still for her? Maybe it wasn't her lack of confidence in her writing skills that stopped the correspondence. Maybe it was a lack of equal conversation. I wish I would have thought about that back then. It must have sounded insensitive of me to run on and on about my life in New York, while she may have had no changes in Pineville to share with me.

 Uncle Shot did his best to keep me from collapsing, but my body slipped through his arms. John Brown stepped in to assist him and they carried me to the back of the church.

My tears and body tremors continued for most of that day and the next. I lay in bed and wouldn't go downstairs, even to eat. I called Chacho on the second day of my isolation, and he was as crazy as ever.

 "Alright," he sighed. "Your mail is piling up and someone even sent you some yellow roses, which, by the way, look just beautiful on my mantle. Are you coming home this week? You are aware of the fact that my fall selection show is scheduled for this weekend and I don't see how I could possibly get through it without you."

He went on for minutes before he realized that I was not engaging in the banter. When he did stop talking, I started crying.

He was perfectly quiet. The only sound was background music—John Coltrane playing the sax in smooth low tones. Had it not been for that, I would have thought we'd lost our connection. After composing myself, I talked about what I thought, how I felt, and why I hurt. He listened. A half hour into our call, my head hurt, and I needed to lie down. I said goodbye and hung up. He understood what I needed. Just like he always did.

"Sissy," Lovely whispered to me one day during our fourth summer together. She was picking up one of our earlier conversations, fooling with the hem of her dress that had come loose weeks ago. "You sure your mama don't drink shine?"

"No, Lovely," I answered while attempting to crack open a pecan with a rock. "My mother don't drink shine."

She stopped fiddling with her hem and looked at me with concern. "I wish my mama didn't. She gets awful mean when she does. Most times she either sleeps too much or stays gone too much. She even came out on the porch with her dress half open when Peanut, Shem Moore's cousin, came by to ask if he could go out with me."

I planted my hands squarely on my hips.

"Peanut Moore came to court you? You never told me that!" I was yelling. I threw down the pecan and the rock to show my disappointment.

"Oh, he ain't nothin'. He tried to court Linda and Sheila from my school, too. I ain't studyin' him."

Just then we heard voices down the road. We had been sitting in the tall grass down by the old cart most of the day, and now the sun was taking its place alongside the earth. I was surprised that my grandmother had not called me in yet, but I wasn't going in until she did. As the voices got closer, we could see that it was Ms. Rose and some man in ugly red plaid pants stumbling down the road toward the bridge. Her mother caught sight of us, although we had tried to dip down low in the green reeds.

"Lovely," her mother sang out. "Come help your mama to the house so this young gentleman can be on his way." Lovely closed her eyes and dropped her head as if doing so might make her or Ms. Rose disappear.

"Come on now, baby," Ms. Rose was getting closer. "This boy here is too young to be seen with a lady like myself."

"You ain't too old for me Rose. Come on now, let me see you to your door."

Ms. Rose and Mr. Ugly Pants were laughing and touching each other in all the wrong places. Ms. Rose almost fell, and Lovely jumped to her feet.

"I'll see you tomorrow Sissy. I need to help my mama."

"See you," I replied, as I got up and turned to walk home. I hoped my answer would always be no when asked if my mama drank shine. I also hoped that Lovely's would be too, one day.

I knew that I could no longer stay in the bed. I needed to make plans for my trip home. I managed to pull on some clothes when my mother knocked softly on the door and entered. We sat on the bed and talked. I shared my regret that I had not realized earlier in my life just how much pain Lovely must have been in. Why didn't I notice back then that her life wasn't going the way mine was?

"You were a child," my mother said, gently running her hands across my head. "Wisdom is not awarded to the young, youth is. That's the same for everyone. I was a child once, too." With that, she opened her soul and told me things I never knew.

My mother had known Rose Fletcher growing up, known her well. Rose was a year or two younger than her and lived in the same house she lives in now. Rose was raised by her grandmother Lucy Fletcher. My grandmother and Lucy Fletcher never cared for each other. My grandmother always thought she was better because she had married my grandfather, Cecil, one of the well-to-do Cole brothers. My mother always hated the way her mother treated Ms. Lucy, but nonetheless it put a wedge between her and Rose.

The year my mother turned sixteen, she got pregnant. My grandmother, of course, was appalled, and ashamed. She was concerned about what Pastor Green and the rest of the church would say. But it was too late. A few people in town already knew. This made her even more enraged. It didn't matter who the father was, and she dismissed my mother when she attempted to explain her love for Ezra Morris, a farmer's son who attended the same church. My grandfather was still alive back then. He had recently fallen ill and didn't have enough strength to fight for his baby girl. He would have never sent his daughter away.

Mom stopped there for a minute, pulled a tissue from her pocket and wiped her tears. I was stunned but could not let on for fear that she would stop talking. I never discussed my chance meeting with Ezra. Why would I? I didn't talk about men with my mother much. More than that, I had always been told that my father's name was Roosevelt Dodd, entrepreneur, businessman, owner of Dodd's Pawnshop on 110th Street in New York. Mama continued.

My grandmother moved with haste in making the arrangements for my mother to live with her aunt in New York. One evening while she was out gathering a few more things to pack for the trip, my mother and Shot finally had a chance to talk. My mother didn't want to leave. She explained all the plans Ezra had made for them. Shot then revealed something that hurt my mother and more thoroughly explained why her mother would not allow her and Ezra to consider marriage. Rose Fletcher was also carrying Ezra's child. The Coles and the Fletchers would have no link, nothing that cast them in the same light, nothing that made them appear to be equal. She chose to send my mother away in order to quiet the gossip of nosy neighbors, but also to save her daughter more pain. Let the hammer fall on Lucy Fletcher and her loose daughter Rosalie. Some weeks later my mother left to live with her Aunt Helen in New York. By this time, she was ready to leave. She knew there would be no farm, no little house in Pineville, no Ezra and Arlene.

My mother stared at me as if the story ended there. I couldn't hold my breath any longer and the words burst from my belly.

"Mom, Lovely was my sister? Roosevelt Dodd wasn't my daddy?"

She finished her revelation. Not long after arriving in New York, she met Roosevelt Dodd in his father's pawnshop, and they began to date. It didn't matter to him that she was pregnant with another man's child. Before she could stop herself, she was in love. They were married within three months, and I was born three months later. Roosevelt died of pneumonia before I turned two. As for Rose and Ezra, they had Lovely.

The events my mother revealed that night were more than my mind could hold. People were not who I thought they were. Not one, not two, but three. The words took a while to seep in. I sat there quietly with my eyes closed and pictured them all.

First was Roosevelt Dodd. Although I had never met my father, I loved him through photographs. His image and stories of his love for us had always been part of my life. Pictures of him were everywhere. One of him in his army uniform on our living room mantle, one of him standing behind my mother holding her around the waist graced my bedroom nightstand. Two hung on the wall of my grandmother's living room along with the other family photographs. My mother had always reassured me of his love and of how proud he would have been of the woman I'd become. I opened my eyes and looked at her.

"He may not have been my father by birth," I said. "But one thing is settled in my heart. I'm not a Morris or a Cole. I am a Dodd."

Second was Ezra Morris. What I thought had drawn me to him wasn't attraction; it was connection. My mother had loved him, and he destroyed her young heart. In my thirty years on earth, I had learned a thing or two about love. Hurt can't make you let it go, shame can't help you shake it off, but another love, a true love, can totally erase it. Ezra had never been anything to me but a stranger on a plane. He had never been anything to Lovely other than the father she never knew. Ezra Morris had no place in my life and never would.

And, third, there was Lovely, my sister. If I had learned at ten years old that Lovely was my real blood sister, would our relationship have been the same? Would we have acted differently, shared differently, loved differently? Would we have fought harder to be together more? The only photograph I had of her was way back in New York. I wanted so badly to look at that photo now. How come I never noticed a resemblance? Was there one? Did my eyes sparkle like hers? Did my voice sing?

I wanted scream, cry, stomp. My mother reached across and held my hand. I counted to ten in my mind so that I would not withdraw it. A wedge between the two of us would serve no good purpose. She was my mother. She was a child herself when she found out about the pregnancy. Choices were made for her. She lived under the shadow of my grandmother all the way into adulthood. She would never have told me if it meant defying her mother. Did Uncle Shot try to help us have a friendship, even though he knew it wasn't his place to tell me the truth? I knew that it would take months to digest it all. I would replay every summer over and over in my head to see if there were clues that I missed. Something said? Something done? I realized all of that might lead me to nowhere different. The thing that haunted me most was whether or not Lovely knew.

"Cecely you can't just bring people into my house unannounced," my grandmother said through clenched teeth. "You know how I am about strangers."

"Grandmom," I replied from my seat at the dinner table.

"Lovely is not a stranger. I have known her for three years now. And you know Ms. Rose. Hasn't she lived down the road from you all her life?"

Earlier that day when my grandmother returned from church, she saw Lovely and me leaving the house through the screen door. She avoided my glance as she exited her car and went around to the back, but I knew I would hear about it later.

"Three years of knowing somebody doesn't mean you can trust them," she replied as she gathered plates from the table. "She's bound to turn out like her mama, and I don't want you getting tangled up in that mess. I saw Lovely more than once this spring with different boys from around here. Now what do you suppose that will lead to?"

I looked into my plate and slipped my fork into a potato. I would respect my grandmother, but I didn't have to agree with her.

"Well?" she pushed.

"Nothing," I said, scooping a few lima beans onto my fork. "Nothing."

The next day we were playing jacks on a sheet of ply board Uncle Shot supplied. Every time Lovely threw up the tiny red ball, she asked another question.

"You don't have no boyfriends up there in New York yet?"

"Nope," I said, grabbing the jacks after she missed. "They all act too silly. Always trying to look up somebody's skirt or hit you on the behind. I don't like that stuff."

"You better catch up."

"Catch up how?" I asked passing the jacks back to her after my miss.

"You almost a woman Sissy. You gonna be fifteen in a minute, and you ain't even kissed a boy," she taunted.

I felt my face get hot. For the first time since I knew her, Lovely made me feel uncomfortable.

"Why are we talking so much boy talk? Come on and concentrate on the game. You had all winter to practice and you ain't no better."

Lovely stood up and leaned against the porch column. "I been practicing other things." She held her hand over her mouth to hide a grin.

"Lovely Rose Fletcher! Are you messin' with boys?" I was on my feet now, too. I wanted to know, and then again, I didn't.

"I ain't tellin' nothin'. My mama says good girls don't tell!" Her voice was getting louder and I looked over my shoulder for signs of Uncle Shot. I looked her straight in the eye.

"Forget the telling part, Lovely. Good girls don't do! Didn't your mama ever tell you that? Good girls don't do!"

The first uncomfortable feeling was followed by a second one. It caught me off guard. Her face slowly began to change. Her eyes became angry and she forced the jacks and the ball from my hand.

"Sissy Dodd, I know you're a favorite girl. Granddaughter of Cecil Mack Cole and Freddie Cole, the most uppity folks ever lived in this town. Daughter of Arlene Cole Dodd, a special girl who moved to the big city. But I got news for you, there's a whole lot more things to be 'shamed of than drinkin' shine. And no, I ain't crazy! I know I asked you more than once if your mama did it and you said no every time! But if I can tell you my mama ain't perfect, seems like you could do the same. She can't be! Nobody's mama is. And ain't nothin' wrong with boys either. If both our mamas wasn't messin' with boys, neither of us would be here!"

Before I could catch my breath, she huffed away and left me quivering and in tears.

When we finished talking that day, my mother and I hugged each other tightly. As she cried in my arms, I felt years of secrets and shame lift from her shoulders. She had always tried to do what was best for me, and not having Ezra Morris as a father was best. On the way home on the plane, I wondered if Lovely ever found out who her father was. Had she ever met him in all those years? And then I remembered my dreams. Lovely, standing on my grandmother's porch as if to demand an answer to a question. Ms. Rose telling her that nothing would change. Did Lovely find out that we were sisters? Did Ms. Rose finally tell her? Did all this have something to do with her death?

I arrived back in New York and took a cab home. I was still feeling low and my eyes gave away the fact that I had been crying for days. When I entered my apartment, Chacho was sitting on the couch. On the coffee table were a stack of rented movies, two large bowls of popcorn, and a couple of ice-cold Diet Cokes. He walked over, hugged me long and tight, and then without warning, snatched a piece of luggage from my hand.

"You know I'm going to have to inspect each piece for damage, right?" he said while grabbing the other one off the floor.

I laughed. I hadn't laughed in days. Chacho could make me feel better without even trying. I once knew someone else who could do the same thing.

I was glad to be back in New York with my friend. I'd brought back two things that were too valuable to leave in Pineville. Chacho's luggage, and my sister, Lovely.

RIGHTEOUS

Why someone would choose to name their child "Righteous" always puzzled my sister Belle. I guess she was afraid he would have a lot to live up to with a name like that. And maybe she was right. But more than that, what stuck in Belle's craw was how someone could name their child Righteous and then leave him on a doorstep.

"What kind of example of righteousness is that?" she would ask as she walked around the house doing this or cooking that.

But even with all that fussing, we decided early on not to change his name. We figured it was what God wanted and just let it be.

My sister and I have lived in this little house on Percy Street our whole lives. Our daddy, Jimmy Everlight Jr., built it with his own hands—him and his brother Jody. Uncle Jody was a heavy drinker. Based on what we heard, he drank more than he built, but Daddy always gave him credit for his hand in it. The house is nestled comfortably between two others much like it. Two-story homes with simple porches sitting back from the street. Maybe not much to some, but everything to us.

Belle often asked, "What would possess a person to put that child on our stoop? Our house don't look like we got plenty of money!" I never questioned the person's decision to choose our home. I say it was the love inside that drew them here.

Righteous arrived on April 22, 1970, in a cardboard box lined with newspaper and covered with a dingy white sweater. Written on the side of the box in big red letters were the words: THIS CHILD'S NAME IS RIGHTEOUS SOUL. I would have loved to have had a camera that day. After discovering the box, Belle jerked backward, startled more because of the name than because of the baby. I still have a good laugh about that to this day. She doesn't like it, but it sure was funny!

After we looked him over closely, made sure all of his limbs were intact, and debated his approximate age, we decided he was about three months old. Belle said the obvious signs were that he wasn't teething and couldn't sit up on his own. I'm still not sure how she knew to look for those things. Neither Belle nor I had children of our own, never raised nobody else's children, and never watched nobody's either.

On that first day while Belle was on the telephone telling every member of the Most Holy Redeemer senior choir that we had a baby visiting, I was busy studying Righteous. I sat him firmly on my lap, held him tightly around the middle and looked deep into his dark brown eyes.

"Where you come from, boy? Who's your mama? Where's your daddy?" I didn't say any of this aloud. I knew his ears were tender and his heart was, too. When I looked at him all I said to him was, "You are a wonder. You are safe right here with me and Belle. God has plans for you." And with that, he smiled.

My sister and I were raised by loving and hardworking parents. There were rules to follow in our house, chores to do, manners to mind, Sunday and weekday school to attend. Nobody could ever say Jimmy and Lettie Everlight's girls were sassy mouthed, fast, unchurched or uneducated. My father was a bricklayer and mama stayed at home. Daddy didn't want his daughters coming home to an empty house in the evenings or being a burden to neighbors. Mama went over our studies with us daily, prepared warm suppers and spent her nights in the arms of a loving husband. Yes, we grew up bound by a circle of love and commitment. If our parents had a disagreement, as we grew older, we may have sensed it but never heard it. Their grown folk conversations were private and spoken in hushed tones behind closed doors.

This house has been known for its love for a long time, and

so it would seem fitting that someone who needed love would find it here. In the months following his arrival, Righteous was gazed upon, rocked, sung to and held. When the choir members brought us a few baby things that first week, we decided to tell them that Righteous was a cousin's child, visiting for just a while. I hated to tell this lie and asked God to cover that sin with all the others.

Righteous grew strong, and boy, did he grow fast! No sooner had I made him a pair of pants than I found myself taking out the hem. When he was three, we began to teach him to read and then to write. By the time he was five, he would read the newspaper to us in the parlor each evening. He asked if he could shorten his name, said it was way too long and took too much time to write. Belle and I gave it some thought and just as quickly dismissed it. He could change it when he was of age. Then it would be his decision alone. Righteous knew neither of us were his mama. Oddly enough, although he played with the children who lived along Percy Street, and all of them had a mother and a father, questions about his parents never came up. Once I heard him tell smart-mouthed Johnny Brown from next door that he didn't need no drunken daddy like his or a swearing mama either. What he had suited him fine. I wasn't happy about him being mean to that poor child, but I knew Johnny must have said something to provoke it.

It was around this time that both Belle and I began to sec-ond-guess our own decisions not to have families. She made her decision on her own. She never married. She never even dated when we were coming up. Belle liked things her way and didn't have the patience for sharing or compromising. We both went to college in Atlanta and Belle came right back home to take care of our dying mother. I did not return home. I had not finished my studies yet, but Belle made sure my mother felt loved and protected until the moment she shut her eyes and went on to glory. Daddy was there, held up by the strength of God and the encouragement of a now sober Uncle Jody. The night my mama died, she was in the bed wrapped up in the arms of her husband, just like she had been every night since they were married. Yes, Lettie Everlight lived and died in love.

One spring evening while we rocked together on the porch and listened to the sounds of Righteous and the other children playing in the distance, Belle told me that she was afraid to attempt a duplication of our parents' affection. She believed it was impossible and if that were so, then it wasn't worth the worry. I, on the other hand, wanted that kind of love so bad, I could taste it. I used to watch my parents from the hall as they held one another close and danced in the parlor. I would see them steal kisses and share what they thought were private giggles.

I longed to be loved like that one day. And to that end, just after I returned from Spelman College, I did find myself in the company of a young man from our church named James. All the girls wanted him. He was supposed to be a catch. At least that's what they told me. Mama was no longer with us, and Belle, although a year older, had no experience with men. I wish I had someone I could have asked. That catch of a man turned out to be a dream-crushing nightmare. Before I knew it, I had compromised everything my parents taught me and am still regretting it. I laid down with him, showed him my soul, and promised my heart. All that didn't matter though. He was lying down with quite a few young girls at church. I found out quickly enough to slap his face one Sunday morning right up in the choir loft, but not soon enough to avoid getting pregnant. I was a plumb fool and now live with internal scars to prove it. Because I was afraid to tell my daddy, I took the advice of others and tried to end the pregnancy.

I guess I must have thought God couldn't see me. No, I truly believed God couldn't see me, or I never would have attempted such a thing. I won't give the details about it; I'll just say that the damage left me hospitalized with blood poisoning, unable to ever bear children again, and no longer my daddy's little girl.

The shame of all that made me choose never to pursue relationships with men or, more honestly, to outright run from them. So, there we were, two aging sisters with no husbands—no one to dance with in the parlor or steal kisses from. But at least God had given us Righteous.

I am unsure which day impacted our lives more, the warm spring morning Righteous arrived, or the cold winter night Ruthie Jean Randolph did. The September before, Righteous had entered the first grade. Belle and I both taught at Dred Scott Elementary for many years, so although he had no birth certificate, the principal, Geraldine Toomer, who had once been a student of ours, allowed him to attend. Miss Dawson, the first-grade teacher that year noticed the resemblance right away, but chose to keep the observation to herself. She decided to seat the children in alphabetical order by their first names in an effort to memorize them.

So there, in the third row, the one that ran in a straight line from her desk to the back of the room, sat two little boys, one behind the other. They looked exactly alike. Rebellious Randolph and Righteous Everlight. She later recounted to the principal how she was distracted those first few days, as thoughts about the boys' obvious relation occupied her mind. The names alone were disturbing enough. After the first week of school, she began to wonder if the other students noticed, but since the two boys dressed, spoke and behaved so differently, the children seemed to pay it no attention.

When picture day came the photographer instinctively reached for the shoulders of these two young boys and placed them front and center in the class photo. Miss Dawson was inclined to lean in and rearrange the setting but she stopped short of actually doing it.

Weeks later, after Righteous brought the class picture home, I imagined that just as Belle and I sat at the kitchen table seeking out our little first grader, that little boy's parents must have been doing the same. Belle reared back in just the same way she had the day Righteous arrived. This time it wasn't funny. Righteous was a very smart boy and so we had to choose our words and methods wisely when trying to figure this thing out. We had him play a game to show us how well he knew his classmates. He stood straight and tall, just as we had taught him, and recited the names of all twenty-five children. When he got to Rebellious, we watched him real close as if expecting something earth shattering to occur, but it didn't. He said that name just like all the others, clear, crisp and with perfect diction, just like we had taught him.

Belle and I held our breath for days, and before we knew it, two months had passed. Apparently, Rebellious' parents had not purchased the class picture, but one day during a visit to the school about his behavior, his mother saw it hanging on Miss Dawson's wall. Ms. Toomer told us that his mother had stormed into her office and began asking a lot of questions that she could not answer. It was that class visit that prompted Ms. Toomer to initiate a conversation with the boys' teacher and then immediately forewarn us.

We were startled by loud pounding on our door late one Friday evening. It was an unfamiliar sound that caught us off guard. No one had ever pounded on the door of 355 Percy Street before. Not even before we lived alone, when my Daddy was alive. After Mama passed, Daddy mostly stayed home. Uncle Jody had gone off to Washington, D.C., to live with some woman he met at a friend's wedding. Our house was quiet with Daddy, Belle, and me living there. After Daddy's hands began to curl and stiffen with arthritis, Belle and I became the breadwinners. It's hard to lay bricks when your hands can't open. For us, the responsibility was not a burden, but an honor. We had the opportunity to give back the love and provision that Daddy had so generously showered on us. We cooked for one another, cleaned the house together on Saturday mornings and rocked on the porch when the evening weather permitted. We had more than enough love among us, and when Daddy went on to join our mother in heaven, he did so quietly and without announcement. We thought he was taking a long nap, when actually he had taken an eternal one. Now he was probably holding my mother again, just like old times. No, this house has never seen nothing but peace and love, so when Ruthie Jean came knocking on our door, she must not have realized that neither Belle nor I were about to let her change that.

I rose from the couch to see what all the fuss was about, but Belle came stomping out of the kitchen and flagged me back into my seat with dish towel in hand, and made her way to the door. I could feel the cold air enter the house right along with our visitors. But it was more than the cold weather that gave me the shivers that night; it was the coldness of a human heart. Belle feigned amazement the first time she laid her eyes on Rebellious in the flesh. He stood next to Ruthie Jean, and although it was dark outside, Belle said Ruthie somehow managed to cast a large shadow across him. About the same time I rose to join them, Righteous came running down the stairs. I truly believe it took this occasion for both boys to realize that the child they had shared a classroom row at school with, was more than just a classmate.

I guess I always expected this day would come. The day we would have to face someone or something from the past related to Righteous. I just never imaged it would be like this. It seemed that Belle and Ruthie Jean were locked in a stare, so I gathered the boys and shooed them off into the kitchen to enjoy some fresh baked cookies and milk.

I wanted to shield the children from as much unnecessary information as possible, so I remained in the kitchen and entertained them with small talk. Rebellious looked just like Righteous. I knew every inch of Righteous, and there was nothing I could see in this child's features that was different. His eyebrows were just as bushy, his eyes just as dark. His little fingers reached for another cookie in just the same way, and when they lifted their glasses to take a sip of milk, they both wet their lips in expectation.

My trance was broken for a moment by the rising pitch in the voices from the other room. Belle had always been the one to take care of business in our house. She had taken on the role of mother to me a long time ago, so it was only fitting that she deal with the threat that crossed our threshold. The voices quieted just enough for me to turn my attention back to what I could now never deny as two brothers. I allowed them to help me place the next batch of dough on the baking sheet and gave them candy sprinkles and powdered sugar from the cabinet to use as decorations. I listened to them talk and watched them laugh while the same dimple formed in their left cheeks.

In those twenty or so minutes, I also began to see their differences, but they were not physical. They were the result of upbringing—nature versus nurture, so to speak. Rebellious was loud, boisterous and controlling. Righteous was polite, calm and caring. Rebellious had worn out shoes with frayed laces, a month's worth of dirt under his fingernails, and coughed on the cookies without covering his mouth. All these things were in dramatic contrast to Righteous' appearance and manners. I heard Ruthie Jean call to her son that it was time to go, so I quickly wrapped him up a few cookies and walked him into the parlor. The tension in the room was weighty. Belle had obviously managed to control the situation and make sure the children didn't get an ear full of grown folks' talk, but bad blood had boiled over in that room for sure.

As soon as they left and the door was shut tight for the night, warmth returned to our parlor. Belle went into the kitchen to clean up, and I hurried Righteous off to a tub of hot water. I didn't mean to, but I scrubbed his skin extra hard. I even allowed him to play with his toy soldiers in there a little longer than usual to make sure no dirt was hiding beneath his fingernails. He was put to bed a bit earlier than usual that night and I explained that it was not a punishment, but that Belle and I had some discussing to do.

We raised our son with as much truth as we thought was appropriate for a young child, and so it was no use acting like the event had not occurred. I got down on my knees next to him, as one of us had done every night since he was old enough to talk, and bowed my head while he prayed.

"Dear God, thank you for this day's portion of mercy and grace. Please watch over us while we sleep. Thank you for food, our home, and our family. Bless Belle, Beanie, my teacher Miss Dawson and most of all, Rebellious. Amen."

Mama passed away early in our adult lives, but we carried with us what she taught us as children. She would talk about diplomacy, respect for one's self and others, and even love for those who may not necessarily love you. Belle had to reach down deep for all those values when dealing with Ruthie Jean Randolph. She also had to rely on her teaching from Mama about how a lady should talk and how to keep peace when what others really wanted was war. I think Belle did one hell of a job. An outsider to the situation would have never known all that verbal tussling was going on. I knew though. I knew because as much as Belle was apprehensive in the beginning about keeping Righteous, as much as she tried to get me to agree to look for his parents, in time it was evident that Belle would kill a rock, cripple a stick, and drown a drip of water when it came to that child.

After putting Righteous to bed, I found Belle seated on the couch in the parlor. She had a tray of tea and cookies ready for us. This was a tradition in our house. Whenever matters of great importance were to be discussed, the family sat in the parlor over tea and cookies to work it out. We did it when Mama died and Daddy couldn't decide whether to bury her here in Virginia, or to allow her sisters to take her back to Charleston, South Carolina, where her other family members were laid to rest. It was unanimous: she was buried right here with us, not more than a mile away, behind St. Luke's Baptist where she attended church as a child. We also did it when Uncle Jody didn't have enough money to get a fake eye. He lost it in a fight with one of his old drinking buddies down at Trudy's Bar. The man was mad when Uncle Jody stopped at one drink and would not continue on for "old time's sake."

Daddy was still working at the time and Belle and I both had decent teaching jobs. It was decided that only Daddy would contribute. He felt his daughters shouldn't pay for the sins of their elders. Daddy paid half and we are still not sure where Uncle Jody got the rest, but that was that. Of course, this parlor was also the place where more than six years ago, Belle and I made up our minds that Righteous was a gift from God, and that you don't give those kinds of gifts back. There were also times our parents did this ritual in our younger days, but we were not invited. We had our two or three cookies before bed, but when Daddy sat in that parlor and Mama put the water on for tea, we knew we were going to bed early that night.

Belle got right to it. She didn't mince words when it came to things like this. Her plump face was shining in the lamplight and she keep smacking her thigh and pulling down on her apron whenever her voice rose. She made me promise not to interrupt until she got it all out, which was hard. I had questions and tried to make a mental note of them until she was finished. So there I sat across from my older sister and allowed her to recount what happened earlier that evening.

No sooner had I walked away with the children, than Ruthie Jean Randolph introduced herself to Belle and communicated the reason for her visit. Although she didn't know they were attending the same school, she had known all this time that Righteous was here with us. She just wanted to make it plain that she had no intention of taking care of two of her sister's unwanted children and didn't want us getting ideas of palming Righteous off on her.

During this time Belle had a chance to take in the young woman. Really give her the once over. She couldn't have been more than twenty-five. Her clothes were too tight, and too short, but they weren't dirty. That made Belle mad right there because she was dressing herself better than she did Rebellious. Quite a few times during her story, Ruthie Jean had to choose her words carefully so as not to curse under someone else's roof, but Belle could tell that she probably cursed just about every other word on a regular basis. When she did let a curse word slip, Belle said she just raised her brow and gave her that same look Daddy used to give Uncle Jody in his drinking days. Those days when my uncle was prone to cussing, but knew it would not be tolerated at our house.

Ruthie Jean went on to say that her little sister Rainelle delivered those babies by herself, and after showing them to Ruthie Jean the next morning, she took off with her boyfriend and never returned. She didn't know what to do, but since their mother was deaf, and their father stayed in the streets day and night, she and her brother had to care for the boys in secret. After a few months, it got to be too much. Her brother wanted to go off to Chicago with some friends, and she didn't think it was fair to stop him. So about the time the babies were three months old, she decided to give one away. Now this is where my questions began to form, but I held my peace.

Her father's name was James Randolph. He and his wife started late having children. When he sat down to tell his daughters about the birds and the bees, he told them about a young girl named Beanie Everlight, who he got pregnant when he was younger. He told them how he paid her no mind when she told him the news and how he left her to figure it out on her own. Their father recited this story to them many times, and each time, he did it he cried harder. It wasn't until he had grown older and wiser that he realized what that tragedy must have done to a woman's soul. It wasn't until he had daughters of his own that he recognized the gravity of the error he had made. Ruthie Jean never forgot that story, even when her father basically abandoned the family and came home when he felt like it. So deciding where to leave the baby was not a hard decision.

Belle stopped there for a moment and allowed me to catch my breath. She asked me if I was alright, and I nodded my head yes. Tears were dropping straight from my eyes onto my house dress. They never got the chance to roll down my face. I gave her the OK, and she continued.

Although their father had no idea his youngest daughter was

with child, he always used to say that Rainelle was struggling with two things deep inside of her; a righteous spirit and a rebellious soul. He said that about her until the day she left. So it was Ruthie Jean who had decided on those names. She'd asked her father whatever happened to Beanie Everlight. He never asked her why she was asking. Ruthie Jean left the baby on the doorstep and moved in with a good friend across town. She never believed the two boys would cross paths this early in life because she felt sure Righteous would attend Benjamin Banneker Elementary, which was near our home and not Dred Scott. When she saw the two boys in the class picture, she thought we were up to something and wanted to make it known that she didn't want no parts of Righteous. Now this is where my sister raised her voice with Ruthie Jean, but just enough to get her point across.

Belle said she spoke as plainly as she knew how when she straightened Ruthie Jean out. She told her how sorry she was that a burden like this had befallen a woman of her age and due to no fault of her own. She assured her that her father was right. He had absolutely no idea what it had done to my soul when I was told that I would never bear children. She informed her that we had no intention of palming Righteous off on anyone. He was a gift from God, and you don't give back those kinds of gifts. Furthermore, this was a house of peace and love. She and Rebellious were welcome to be a part of it, but Ruthie Jean or nobody else was going to divide it. She told her that over the last two months we were frightened that she would try to stake a claim on our child, but now, looking at Rebellious' condition we were inclined to stake a claim on hers. My sister can be too blunt at times, but she didn't speak with a forked tongue. If she said that, she meant it.

She told Ruthie Jean that by the way she had dressed and raised Rebellious, it looked like the one child was just as much burden as the two would have been. And then she hit me with it. You know how when you're expecting something bad and something good is thrown at you. I lifted my head and Belle held my face in her hands.

She said, "Beanie, I told Ruthie Jean to leave Rebellious with us. I told her we had enough love for both of them and then some. I let her know that although we were up in years and no stranger to sorrow, we were well acquainted with the blessings of God and that if she could not raise that child in love, then we would be glad to. And Beanie, guess what she said?"

I didn't want to guess, and Belle didn't make me. The next morning Rebellious arrived much the same way as Righteous did. Ruthie Jean left him at our doorstep with a box full of clothes and sped off in a car just as I opened the door. Unlike Righteous, we decided to call Rebellious by another name until he was old enough to make the decision for himself. We allowed him to select it. He decided on James, after his grandfather. Now we had a job to do. We had to raise these boys right, teach them right, and love them right. And we did so with each day's portion of God's mercy and grace. When all was said and done, God gave us double for our trouble!

THE STATION

It was a warm spring afternoon, the type of day that showcases its true beauty after a nice long rain. When I arrived at the train station, it wasn't very crowded. I am accustomed to traveling alone for work and had never been to this station before. For the first time since I can remember, I hoped that someone would be joining me. There wasn't the normal hustle and bustle that I had encountered at 30th Street Station in Philly or Grand Central in New York. Here the people were much calmer, more pleasant. Their faces were not twisted with worry or scowling with impatience.

There was an older balding gentleman sitting on the bench just across from me. I thought I recognized him. He favored an elderly neighbor from the street I grew up on, but I wasn't quite sure if it was him. I smiled when I caught his yellowed eyes and he grinned widely back at me. I hadn't expected such a spirited response. He was at least 75 years old with a mustache and close-cut beard. I could tell he was short because as he sat, his feet barely skimmed the worn linoleum floor. He wore a crisp pale yellow, button-down shirt and hard-pressed khakis. I glanced down at his brown shoes. They appeared to be spit shined. I couldn't help but think that he likely had an attentive and loving wife at home, who helped him dress this morning.

Next to me, a small boy sat wide legged on the floor playing with a red Hot Wheels car. With no announcement, he hoisted himself up from the floor, using my knee to steady himself. Before I knew it, the micro-sized red Mustang was rolling up my forearm, across my stomach and back down the other arm, stopping abruptly at the cuff of my blouse. The boy squealed as he retrieved his vehicle and started the journey again. I was surprised by how comfortable he was with a stranger, and in spite of being used as a race track, I was happy to take part in his joy. Up one arm, across, down the other, up one arm, across, down the other. This went on a few more times and although he was no worry to me, I began to wonder where his parents were. I looked around at the other passengers to try to determine who they could be. He appeared to be cared for very well. His face shined and his hair was neatly cut. Clothes impeccably matched but rumpled, just as you would expect for a small child.

I smiled when the little boy wandered over to a young girl with dark curly hair sitting further down on the same bench as me. I leaned forward slightly to get better view of her. She wore knee high socks and a plaid skirt, Oxford shoes, and a cardigan. Surely, I thought to myself, she is much too young to be the boy's mother. Without warning, the boy began to use her as a human racetrack, just as he had with me moments before. Up one arm, across, down the other. I watched her face first reflect amusement, then curiosity and finally discomfort. She began to twist in her seat, as if trying to see who this child might belong to. She looked over at the older man, and he stared back blankly. When our eyes met, I smiled warmly and shrugged my shoulders. By then, the little boy had abandoned his game with her and moved on.

I heard the tiles on the railway information board begin to turn over and flap rapidly. I shifted my attention to the board to read the arrival and departure updates. Oddly, there were no arrivals listed; that much I could see even without my glasses. And where were my glasses? I squinted hard to make out the departures, and from what I could read, they all said the same thing. That didn't make much sense to me, so I stood up and walked over to get a closer look. Over and over, row after row, every hour on the hour, the same destination was listed: HOME.

I don't remember telling my husband that I was traveling for work today. I started my morning like any other. I got up, dressed, and headed out for the forty-five-minute drive to work. My husband was working the night shift this week, so we would miss seeing each other by just an hour. Normally, in the evenings when I got home, dinner would be ready and we would sit down to a quick meal for two. We'd share a kiss, a smile, a joke, the news for the day. Sometimes he would lay in bed with me until I fell asleep. I liked that. Last night he made smothered chicken. Mmm... He sure can cook. Just the thought of him made me reach for my phone to call. Where was my phone? That was strange. I scanned the station searching for a pay phone. No luck. First my glasses, and now my phone. I looked on the bench for my pocketbook. No pocketbook. I needed to talk to someone. Where was the lost and found?

    I stood up, looking around to see if there was a customer service sign along the walls and noticed that the young girl in the plaid skirt looked anxious, as though she forgot something or someone. She moved to the edge of her seat and began looking around frantically and then, strangely, without warning, she calmly sat back in her seat.

    Something strange was going on. I began to take in the scene a bit more closely and made some unsettling observations. None of us had suitcases—and I don't remember checking one in. Was I going somewhere for a day trip? Was it for work? Why couldn't I remember? I noticed a large window below the baggage check-in sign was covered with a white shade. I guessed that meant baggage service was not available. Also, it appeared the station was no longer filled with people. Just the old man, the little boy, the young girl, me, and two other passengers remained. No one else had entered, and everyone else was gone.

Earlier, while driving to work I listened to my favorite gospel playlist, that one where every song on it lifted my spirit. As I traveled down the road toward Highway 81, I had every intention of getting to work on time. I had meetings scheduled back-to-back and was already looking forward to spending time with my husband that evening. Maybe he would stay in the bed until I fell asleep tonight.

"All aboard!"

The announcement sounded clearly from the speakers. No crackle, no echo. As the train pulled into the station the light from its headlamp illuminated the windows facing the platform. Oddly enough, the little boy was the first to react. Giddy, he suddenly calmed as he put the red car in his pants pocket and headed toward the platform door. The older gentleman ran the palms of his hands along his thighs as if to remove any wrinkles that might have formed while he sat. He stood and reached for my hand. I didn't question the invitation. For some reason it felt natural. The young girl was visibly nervous. As I locked hands with the older man, I reached for hers. I could not hear the train, but the bright light announced its approach. I knew in that moment, that my day would not end as planned. My husband would have to eat without me, but he wouldn't be alone. He would be surrounded by my parents, my siblings, and our friends. As the young girl placed her hand in mine, the little boy ran back and wrapped his arms around the older gentleman's leg. We had formed a physical link and I could feel its weight.

Suddenly, memories of that morning came flooding back and everything became clear.

The roads were wet from the downpours the night before. I approached the last intersection on Linden Boulevard before the road turned into Highway 81. I saw the young girl in the plaid skirt and cardigan at the bus stop just ahead to my right. The light was green.

Just as I reached the light, my stomach began to churn. I imagined my husband cooking at the stove, and turning to smile at me. I glanced out of my driver's side window and saw a black car drive past. The little boy was playing with his red car in the rear window. He must have been kneeling on the seat. He looked at me, and waved as the car drove ahead.

I still had the green light, but my foot was only pressing lightly on the accelerator. A white SUV traveling on the cross street ran the red light. The older man in the yellow shirt was driving and there was a woman about the same age in the passenger seat.

WHAM!

The SUV slammed into the left rear door of the black car. In slow motion, the black car was lifted up from the ground and flew toward my car. I threw up my arms to shield my face and dove toward the passenger seat. As my head dropped below the dashboard all three cars: the white SUV, the black car, and mine all careened sideways toward the bus stop. The young girl in the plaid skirt stood frozen, screaming in horror.

The elderly woman passenger in the SUV never arrived at the station. Could that have been the wife who I imagined helped to dress the older gentleman? The little boy was not escorted to the station by an adult. Had his mother or father been the driver of the black car?

Still linked together, the four of us walked out to the platform. I didn't yearn for more time here. A peaceful satisfaction laid gently on my heart and I smiled at the thought of what would lie ahead. With the light on the platform now still and the engine idling, we boarded the train for HOME.

PAUL AND SILAS

It rained so hard that week, it seemed like the sky would fall. Dark clouds cloaked the sun, and the wind blew with a fierceness I had never known. I was forced to my knees twice as I traveled toward the riverbank. This was the fifth straight day of torrential rain in Hopewell. The storm had run right through southern Georgia, but when it arrived here it decided to stay. That can happen sometimes. You get to places with intentions of moving on and then something makes you linger. Sometimes that thing is good, sometimes bad.

As I slid down the muddy embankment, I could see Silas rocking back and forth on his knees. Moans seeped from his heaving chest, and he stuttered through quivering lips. Dora stepped toward him, but he shoved her away. Silas ripped off his wet coat and wrapped it around his brother. He held him close, shielding his lifeless body from the storm that took his life. I got closer, he turned and looked at me. From that day until this one, I will never forget the pain in his eyes. They screamed out with emptiness. I walked around to the other side of Paul's body. My heart was pounding so hard in my throat that it hurt. I couldn't speak. There were no words. My knees gave way and I fell into the soft, wet earth. Silas shifted Paul's body and placed his head on my lap. I wiped the mud from Paul's face with my hands; then I started to slip away. The sounds of rain and sobbing began to fade. I was no longer on the riverbank. I was home in Virginia, and I was headed for Hopewell.

I had never been to Hopewell before. Never been out of Virginia. Hopewell was the place where my parents were born. The place that they never cared to return to. My father was the son of a preacher and a schoolteacher. That really meant you were somebody in those days. That your family had promise. It was very different for my mother. She was the daughter of an uneducated single woman. My grandmother raised ten children alone. Many of the town's finest, well-to-do men were the fathers of her children, but none would admit it. She was a seamstress and kept her children fed, clothed, and warm. I remember my mother saying that so many times. My dad went to college and when he returned, he earned a good salary working for the government. When my parents met, they fell in love within weeks. My father saved everything he could, and three years later they left Hopewell. My father's parents were undone about his choice for a wife. There was a whole lot of crying at the bus station that day. My parents didn't get married until they reached Virginia, and they never went back to Georgia again.

I was born the following year, 1940. My parents worked hard and raised me and my two brothers in the heart of Richmond. We too were fed, clothed, and warm. Reverence for God, love for family, and getting a good education were all stressed in my home. Each day began with "good mornings" and a big breakfast. We ended our nights with stories about our day and my mother's warm desserts. I never imagined how short our time together would be. There was so much I never had a chance to say.

In May of 1958, the day after my birthday, both my brothers were found hanging from a tree. That's a hard thing. Harder than anything I believed life could have dealt out. If it's hard for you to hear, imagine how hard it was for us to live. If I didn't think it was important to tell, I wouldn't tell it. My brothers were killed because they stood up for me. I told them that some white boys from school followed me home spewing hateful and nasty words. I was sorry I told them as soon as the words left my mouth. I begged them to let it alone, told them that I scared the boys off with threats of what my daddy would do to them, and that it probably wouldn't happen again. I wish I would have told my father instead. A few weeks after the funeral I asked my parents if I could go away for a while. The only place to escape to was Hopewell, Georgia. That's where all their family still lived. Now it was me boarding a bus, running to the same place my parents had once run away from.

The people on the bus were pleasant and kind. I wasn't used to real southern hospitality. The woman I sat next to offered me chicken, lemonade, ham, biscuits, and preserves, out of a large canvas bag under her seat, all while telling me her name and asking me mine. She boarded the bus somewhere south of Virginia and was a proud resident of Hopewell. Before we arrived at our destination, I learned a few important things about the town. My belly was filled with good food, and my head was full of information about people I was yet to meet.

Miss Vettie—that's how she introduced herself—explained that there were good and bad people in Hopewell, just like in any other town. Doesn't matter if the town is big or small when it comes to people's funny-acting ways, or outright shameful behavior. She instructed me on many things. If I was ever short of money and needed groceries, I could count on Mrs. Henderson, from Henderson's General Store. But never Mr. Henderson. He, as she told it, was nasty as a snake and twice as hateful. The local church pastor and his wife were a meek and God-fearing couple who fought like the devil when they thought no one was listening. And then there was a popular girl about my age named Dora Davis, who walked with her nose in the air and a mirror in her pocket. I knew she meant the second part figuratively. My mother used to say that about a neighbor who thought she was better than everyone else. This girl craved attention and despised any other girl who got any.

Miss Vettie went on to tell me she could tell that I was a sweet and well-mannered young lady. She figured that I wouldn't have a problem finding a nice young man to marry off with, if that was my intention. I assured her that getting married off was the furthest thing from my mind, but she still felt I should be warned that all of my admirable qualities would be the reason my first adversary in Hopewell would be

Dora Davis. Before we got off the bus, I thanked Miss Vettie for her kindness and assured her that as soon as I got settled, I would look her up. According to her, my uncle Nate's house was a stone's throw from hers and anyone could direct me there.

✍

I must have sat on that hard green bench for an hour before Uncle Nate arrived. He was a huge man. He appeared to stand about seven feet tall. His clothes were a little tattered and his face was covered with specks of dried mud.

"Eva? Eva Lewis? Is that you?" he said as he came closer. "I'm sorry I had you waitin' so long. We just found out yesterday that you were comin' and I had to close up the shop before I could leave." He quickly grabbed my suitcases, hoisting one up under his arm and grabbing the other with his left hand. He extended his other hand to me.

"Come on now. It's late. Dinner is waitin'." I took his hand and smiled.

My mother described him so well. His voice was deep, like a bear's growl, and his smile revealed a gap at least two teeth wide. I felt a bit nervous riding with this extra-large stranger. I think he recognized it, and quickly began to make me feel comfortable by telling me stories about my mother when she was younger. In no time we were laughing and I began to feel at ease.

As we approached the house, I could see smoke billowing from the chimney. Gray puffs climbed straight up toward heaven as if someone wanted God to get a whiff of their good cooking. Uncle Nate brought the truck to a smooth stop, and I began taking in the beauty of this wondrous place. The white and green house was small and freshly painted. A porch extended all the way across the front, and there were beautiful beds of flowers on either side of the steps. Although the porch chairs didn't match, the cushions did. The windows were clean and sparkling in the fading sunlight. They were trimmed with lace curtains that softly fluttered out of the open windows. Before I could survey more of the area, the screen door suddenly swung open. Out stepped the handsomest boy I had ever seen. Almost as tall as Uncle Nate, skin like warm hot chocolate, and loud. Boy, was he loud! I thought this must be my cousin Jimmy, but I remembered hearing he was away at school. He skipped all four front steps in one leap, and bounded toward the truck with long strides.

"Hey there! My name is Silas. Welcome to Hopewell! Miss Nan had me cleanin' and scrubbin' the back room since yesterday just for you. Come on now! Don't be shy. Jump on down out the truck." He rattled on so quickly, that I didn't get the chance to say hello.

"Boy, if you don't let my niece be. Can't you see she's tired from her trip? Grab them suitcases for me and bring them in the house," Uncle Nate interrupted.

"Yes, Sir," he replied, flashing a brilliant smile.

By this time Aunt Nan was standing in the doorway. Uncle Nate helped me down from the truck and up the few steps to the porch. I was welcomed by my aunt with a warm and gentle squeeze. The way she compared in size to my uncle was almost comical. Only about five feet tall, she was dwarfed by his height. Her hair was long and black, and she wore it pulled back in a long plait. She was wearing a beautiful blue and white dress covered with a matching apron.

The inside of the house mirrored the coziness of the outside. A couch and chair were to the left of the door. A table and four chairs to the right. A few decorative throw rugs warmed up the wood floor. To the far right in the corner, was a stove, sink, and a few cabinets. Dead center on the back wall was a door that separated this part of the house from the bedrooms and bathroom. There were two bedrooms—one for my aunt and uncle—and the other for Jimmy. That's where I would sleep. Silas sat my suitcases down there and brushed past me, headed for the door. I was secretly hoping he wouldn't leave so soon, but Uncle Nate wanted me to have a family dinner with them my first night there. With that, Silas was gone.

We ate and talked and laughed. They seemed happy to have me with them. As Aunt Nan and I washed the dishes, I glanced through the window and saw Silas sitting near the road on a large tree stump.

He seemed to be staring right at me. I quickly pulled the curtain closed and finished my work.

Later that night, I joined them in the living room. My aunt sat on the couch darning socks, and Uncle Nate sat in what seemed to be his regular chair. The rhythmic motion of his rocking chair was soothing to my soul. That first day had passed without tears for me. I only thought of how much I would have loved for my brothers to see this place, to be here with me in Hopewell. In a way, I knew they were.

When I awoke the next morning, the sun seemed to shine brighter than ever. Aunt Nan went for a ride with Uncle Nate and told me to make myself at home. I ate the breakfast she had left for me and quickly washed the dishes. There were a few shirts in a laundry basket next to the ironing board, so I pressed collars and cuffs until the basket was empty. I felt a twinge of loneliness at first, but I was too excited about this new and wondrous place to allow the feeling to last too long. Before noon, I took a walk down the long winding road away from the house. I walked for more than ten minutes before I reached another house. I noticed there was someone sitting on the old unpainted fence. As I got closer, I could see it was the boy from yesterday, loud Silas. He must have been in deep thought because I was very close to him, but he never moved.

"Good morning, Silas," I said from several feet away.

He calmly turned and looked at me, almost as if it was a response to my presence, and not to my greeting. He tilted his head to one side and then the other.

"What's the matter? Cat got your tongue today?"

He smiled sheepishly and lowered his head. Immediately, his smile disappeared. From my experience with him the day before, I was surprised that he didn't want to talk with me, but I quickly remembered there were many days when I didn't feel much like talking.

"Well, bye then," I whispered as I turned on my heels to walk back to the house.

I took in the beauty of the golden corn fields that lined the road. The wind gently blew across the tops of the stalks, and then washed across my face. I was lost in the peacefulness of the afternoon when I heard a noise behind me and looked over my left shoulder to see what it was. I could see the next house a long way off, and Silas was still sitting on the fence watching me. I took a chance and waved. He waved back.

"That's more like it," I thought. Suddenly someone grabbed me from behind.

"Hey Girl! Glorious day for a walk isn't it?" he shouted. It was Silas, walking beside me at a stride that resembled a skip.

"Silas, how did you? I thought you were back there on..." Before I could get all the words out, I turned and saw that the boy I spoke to just minutes ago was still sitting there on the fence. I looked back at Silas, confused.

"Oh, I'm sorry. That's my brother Paul. He doesn't say much. Hasn't ever said much. I guess that's why folks say I'm loud, with him being so quiet and all."

I stood there collecting my thoughts. I looked at him, and then back at his brother, who gave me another wave. I waved back.

"I guess you can see we're twins," Silas continued. "Wherever I go, he's not far away. It's always been that way."

Silas walked me back to the house. He told me that he and Paul were raised by their grandmother. When he was little, his parents moved to Chicago looking for jobs and a better life for the family. They were supposed to come back for them, but never came. Their grandmother was getting along in years and decided to put their house and all the land she owned in her grandsons' names. They grew corn and had orchards of pecan and apple trees. All the corn that stretched between their house and my uncle's belonged to him and Paul. They sold everything they grew in town, but naturally kept Aunt Nan's kitchen stocked.

The brothers were good at fixing cars, building houses, and writing letters. They made a respectable living on all these things. The letters were mostly for older folks who wanted to write back to their children who moved north. Uncle Nate had taken the twins under his wing a long time ago, back when they first started playing stick ball with my cousin Jimmy.

When we finally reached the doorway to the house, and I turned to say goodbye, sure enough there was Paul standing under a large tree in the yard. I never knew he was behind us. His hands were slowly working at a stick or something.

"Does Paul ever speak?" I asked.

"I've never heard him make a sound," answered Silas, looking back over at Paul. "He's quiet but quick. Smarter than anyone I know and twice as strong. Well, enough about me and Paul. How about you and me having a picnic tomorrow? After I come from town in the morning? How's that sound? Do you think Mr. Nate will let you?"

I looked at Silas and smiled. That boy had enough words in his mouth for three people. Him, Paul, and somebody else.

"Yes," I said. "I would love a picnic."

Uncle Nate and Aunt Nan approved of the outing. They were just happy that I was happy. It didn't hurt that they had known Silas most of his life and trusted him like their own son. The next morning after all my chores were done, I made little sandwiches and put ice cold lemonade in drinking jars. I wrapped up some of the cookies Aunt Nan helped me make for dessert the night before and placed everything into a long-handled basket. Silas showed up at noon with a blanket and we went on our way.

We didn't have to walk far—just a few minutes past his house. He picked out a beautiful spot near the river's edge. There was a large tree with branches that stretched wider than I had ever seen. It was draped in luscious green leaves and vibrant pink blossoms. Towering sunflowers lined the bank overlooking the water. We stopped and set up our picnic. The sun beamed strong outside our shaded refuge, and a familiar soft wind was softly blowing. We ate and talked, taking the opportunity to share as much as we could about our lives in Virginia and Georgia, or at least the places within them that we knew. And just as Silas had said, Paul was not far away. I hadn't noticed him when

Silas came to pick me up, but as we strolled down the road, Paul made sounds by scraping sticks in the gravel, or by throwing stones at trees. I could tell it was intentional. I asked Silas about Ms. Vettie, the Hendersons, the pastor, his wife, and Dora Davis. He confirmed it was all as true as she stated and added that Ms. Vettie was the nosiest person in town. We rolled on the blanket laughing.

During the entire picnic, Paul sat a little ways off down river. I offered him a sandwich and some lemonade when we first arrived. He smiled at me, but lowered his head and turned away. As me and Silas talked, Paul tossed rocks into the river, and every now and then, he would look over at us and wave. According to Silas, Paul loved the river, and he wasn't as lonely as he seemed. We now know that wasn't true.

Another week passed quickly. I was helping my aunt make dresses for a wedding and to say we were busy would be an understatement. By the time we ate dinner each night and cleaned up the kitchen, I was dog tired and could barely keep my eyes open. I saw Silas here and there when he and Paul stopped by to work on something with Uncle Nate. There wasn't much time for idle chit-chat as my aunt called it, but he did get a chance to tell me that Paul had been spending a lot of time with Dora Davis. With this announcement I could tell Silas was worried, and even though I had never laid eyes on Dora I can say that I was worried too. That night before bed, I remembered how Ms. Vettie described Dora, and then recounted a few more things about her that Silas had shared. It became clear that Dora Davis was trouble.

By the following week me and Aunt Nan were putting the finishing touches on the dresses. Several fittings with the wedding party had already taken place, and things weren't as hectic. Silas came by every evening and we sat on the porch steps taking in the sunset. Some days Paul was down by the tree, whittling away at a stick. On other days he was nowhere to be found. Silas explained that he was happy his brother was starting to find his own way, but was concerned that the way appeared to be with Dora. According to Silas, before I arrived in Hopewell, Paul wouldn't even so much as look at Dora. The brothers shared the same friends growing up. The boys and girls their age in Hopewell all came up together. Went to school together. Attended-church together. Dora was part of that group. Paul had a good sense of people, and Silas was sure that Paul knew Dora didn't mean anyone any good. So, this sudden shift made no sense to him.

The more I thought about Dora and Paul being together, the less sleep I got. Silas talked about their childhood, telling me stories that made me laugh and a few that made me cry. Each evening I spent on that porch with Silas, I learned as much about Paul as I did about him. When I finally talked to my aunt and uncle about all of this, they helped me to make sense of it all.

"Paul has been watching his brother start to take an interest in you and he probably felt left out," Aunt Nan explained. "No matter how much you try invite him in, Paul knows something is different. He might even feel like an outsider in his brother's life for the very first time."

"Remember Eva," Uncle Nate added. "Just because Paul doesn't talk, it doesn't mean he can't feel. Now all of this is not anyone's fault. You and Silas deserve to care for each other. It's just that life is complicated. Sometimes the very thing that brings happiness to someone can mean sadness for someone else. I'm sure your parents told you what happened when they fell in love. Not everyone was happy about that, and people responded differently."

That's all they said, and it was enough. I tossed in the bed all night wrestling with the fact that happiness for me and Silas, may have caused Paul pain. I had not cried for my brothers since I arrived in Hopewell, but that night I cried for Paul.

Uncle Nate and Aunt Nan took their usual drive into town the next morning, and I decided to plant some flower pots for the porch. When I opened the door, I was startled by Paul standing on the porch steps. Before stepping out I looked both ways up and down the road, but no Silas. Paul looked me in the eyes for the very first time. It is hard to explain. He had a handsomeness that was mesmerizing—very different than Silas—even though they were identical twins. It made my heart warm, but not my conscience. He handed me a small object. After holding it in my hand and running my fingers along the curves, I could see that it was a smooth stick whittled into the shape of a woman. It was very delicate—beautifully hewn. Before I could stop myself, I softly kissed Paul on his cheek. Under his warm brown skin, I could tell he was blushing. The basket Silas and I used for our picnic was on the porch table. Paul looked at me and reached over to touch the handle. I instantly knew what he was asking, but explained that it was a dreary and windy day. We both looked around at things blowing here and there in the yard. I explained that Uncle Nate said a terrible storm was coming. This wasn't a good day for a picnic. Without thinking of Silas, well actually without even thinking, I told Paul that as soon as the sun dried the ground, he could take me on a picnic. He smiled again, though not as brightly as the first time. He turned, jumped off the porch and took off down the road in the direction opposite of his house.

When they returned from their drive, Uncle Nate reported that the storm had torn up a few towns on its way toward Hopewell. As soon as he got all the bags in off the truck, he was going to head over to help Paul and Silas tie a few things down at their house. By the time he returned, a torrential rain had started. The raindrops were hard— the kind that makes noise when it lands on soft earth. When my uncle came through the door, Silas was with him.

"I can't find Paul," Silas said with a bit of fear in his voice.

"He'll show up soon," Aunt Nan said. "Take off that wet coat and have some food with us."

It rained without stopping. We ate, but there wasn't much talking. Silas pushed the food around on his plate and was clearly concerned about his brother. We all were, but tried not to show it.

"I haven't seen him all day," Silas broke the silence. "That's so unusual."

I wanted to keep quiet but knew that I had to say something.

"He was here this morning."

"Here?" Silas asked. "What was he doing here with Mr. Nate in town?" He stood up and looked at me like he knew the answer, but wanted me to say it.

I looked around at everyone and explained what happened earlier that day. I mentioned that Paul wanted to go on a picnic and I left out the gift and the kiss. I don't know why, but even without the whole story, they all seemed to know there was more to it.

"Which way did he go Eva?" Silas said, putting on his damp coat at the same time. I was standing now, realizing that maybe I should have said something sooner.

"He ran towards town."

"Town? More than likely he ran to Dora's, hoping she would go on a picnic with him. She'd be fool enough to do it too, even with the rain coming. If she thought it meant one more gift, or a couple more of his hard-earned dollars, she would pack a basket in a minute."

"Has he ever taken Dora on a picnic before, Silas?" Aunt Nan asked as she walked over to get Uncle Nate's boots for him.

"Not that I know of," Silas replied. His voice was trembling. I knew Paul wasn't back yet, but I still didn't realize why everyone seemed so nervous.

"Come on," said Uncle Nate, resting his hand on Silas' shoulder. "Let's go find him. First we'll go to Dora's so we can hopefully rule out this whole picnic thing."

After they left, Aunt Nan explained that storms didn't come to Hopewell often, but when they did, it was always too much rain. So much rain that the ground couldn't soak it up. Rain that overflowed the riverbanks. Rain that, though needed, often meant trouble.

Uncle Nate and Silas came home well after dark. They'd searched all over for Paul but couldn't find him. No one answered the door at Dora's house. It was still raining. Silas stayed and slept on the couch. The next morning, we all went out to search for Paul. Although it had let up a bit, it was still raining. Uncle Nate got help, and we were joined by Mr. Henderson, the Pastor, and a few other people I had never met before.

Silas and me went back to Dora's house. She stood in the doorway. Tall and beautiful, with light caramel skin and dark eyes. Despite her stunning looks, as soon as she opened her mouth ugly slid out. She leaned against the doorpost and started admiring her nails. She said that Paul came by with a bag full of snacks and some soda pop. He took her down to the river for a picnic.

"Well, where is he now?" Silas practically shouted. Dora wrinkled up her face and put her hand on her hip.

"Silas, you ain't never been to my door, and the one time you can't find your no-talking brother, you on my porch?" Silas took a step toward her, and I placed my hand gently on his arm. At that moment Mrs. Davis walked out onto the porch.

"Dora tell them everything," she said sharply. "Tell them what I heard you tell your sister last night while you thought I was asleep. This boy is looking for his brother!"

And then she told the rest. How they were eating the snacks and drinking the soda pops when it started to rain. How Paul jumped up to gather everything and she was just trying to give him a hug. How she asked him if he had a present for her, but he wouldn't let her dig in his pockets like he usually did. Then she finally persuaded him. She reached in and found a perfect heart whittled smooth like a pebble, but he kept trying to take it back from her. When she realized he hadn't made it for her, she threw it in the river and ran home.

I was watching Silas' face the whole time. He was stuck somewhere between anger and despair. He always knew that Dora didn't really care for Paul, but in an attempt not to hurt him, he never told him. We walked off the porch with the burden of Paul heavy on Silas's shoulders.

Everyone had already searched the riverbank where Dora and Paul had held their picnic. There'd been no sign of him. Silas went back home and stayed, hoping Paul would walk through the door. The next day we decided to start up the search again with Silas in the lead. The rain had eased up a bit. This time when we headed to the river Dora joined us. Her mother insisted. Uncle Nate had gathered everyone again and people went off in all directions. Silas was in front, with Dora close behind. I stayed close to Aunt Nan. After several hours of searching, we were all soaked to the bone.

With each step my heart ached more. I thought of my brothers.

I thought of my parents whom I dearly missed. Most of all, I thought about Paul and Silas, who I'd met at a time when my heart was crushed. In the short time I had known them, they both had helped me to heal. I believed that Silas knew it, but Paul felt it. Love can sometimes come very quickly, even more so when you have an empty space to fill. For Paul and Silas, it was the space that their parents once occupied. For me it was the void left after the loss of my brothers. I realized that I needed Paul just as much as I needed Silas.

A gust of wind knocked me to my knees. I was almost at the river when I heard Dora scream. I managed to push myself up from the mud. Aunt Nan grabbed my arm and tried to hold me back. Slipping in the soft earth, I grabbed at low-hanging branches to keep upright. That's when I saw them.

There was Silas, holding Paul in his strong yet limp arms. The beauty of their identical faces held closely together. Paul was gone and the sound of his brother's pain was deafening. As I laid in the rain-soaked Georgia mud, cradling a boy that I barely knew yet deeply loved, the frailty of life and the suddenness of death once again became real. Dora and the white boys who taunted me back in Virginia lived miles apart. Their lives were vastly different. To many people, unkindness and hatred are not the same, but I can tell you from experience that the consequences are; they both create wounds and the scars remain.

I am still living in Hopewell. Many people have come and gone from my life. Filling emptiness and leaving spaces. I have since married Silas and have one son. His name is Paul.